THE

Prototype

A Story of True Love by

Jamilah Ewing

Special thanks to Ra Communications.

Cover design by Mandie Hungarland
Edited by Rashida Rawls | Ra Communications and Mandie Hungarland

Printed in the U.S.A.

For Dad

TABLE OF CONTENTS

ONE

Rise

leep bleep chingaling bleep bleep chingaling. Damn phone alarm. I reach over to grab my smartphone and see that it's 5:00 a.m. I put the phone back on the nightstand face down and say aloud, "Thank you." I sit all the way up and throw the sheets over to my left, where Carlos used to sleep. He sleeps in his office now since... "The Incident." He should consider himself lucky that I am still married to him after this one.

I lean back onto my pillow for about five minutes before getting up for prayer. With my eyes open I think to myself that this isn't an ordinary day today. Friday, April 5, 2019 is the first day back to the Salon since "The Incident" which happened on March 26, 2019 at approximately 3:02 p.m. I can't stop thinking about it, but I survived and I'm going to power through it all today.

As I roll my legs over to get up, I shake my right hand out because it's always cold and numb in the morning. I have a very serious case of carpal tunnel that I don't—won't—speak about. If my clientele found out, I could lose business. Besides,

I don't want little Ava to think that I'm weak and can't handle pressure.

I drag myself to the restroom to wash up for my morning prayer when I hear a tiny knock on the bathroom door. I grab a towel to wipe my wet face. "Who's that?" I call out.

"It's Ava, Mommy."

I open the door. "Hey little munchkin, what are you doing up?"

"I wanted to make prayer with you and make sure you were okay because I know that you're going back to work today."

I smile and kiss her forehead, "Of course you can join me."

After prayer, I usually sit in the bay window and have coffee alone. Today, I have my concerned 12-year-old daughter keeping me company.

"Ava, can I fix you some oatmeal baby?" I ask.

"No ma'am, I'm just gonna have a cereal bar and some juice," Ava responds.

"Munch, you know I don't mind," I say with a smile as I toss the coffee filter in the trash can.

"It's all good, Mom," she says as she grabs onto me for a quick side hug while I'm preparing breakfast for the boys. She goes to sit at the kitchen table but then turns the dining chair toward me as she eats her granola bar. She watches me like this sometimes. Quietly observing. After about two minutes, I sigh and then give her the side eye just above my glasses.

Slightly annoyed, I ask, "What, Ava?"

"Nothing, Mom," she replies.

"C'mon!" I say as I lay the cooking spoon down and reduce the heat on the eye of the stove.

"Mommy, don't get mad at me for saying this, but I don't think that you should go into the shop today."

I take a seat next to her "Why not, munch? I feel fine."
I put my wrist brace on my right hand for my carpal tunnel.

"Well, that's good; I'm just a little worried. Are you
going to break up with Daddy?" Ava asks, looking at me with
her big brown eyes.

I gasp. "Ava, where would you get that kind of idea
from?" I ask angrily.

Ava hesitates because she doesn't want to upset me.
"Well, we heard you and Dad talking to Cousin Justin about
putting up a GoFundMe for us on his Facebook page, and it's
been a bad week."

"Well no, no, no, baby. I'm good to go! I feel like
myself when I can work. Are you good to go to school? I
mean, the video of me *did* go viral." She looks at me, surprised,
as if I wasn't aware. "I know, Isaiah told me yesterday." I close
my eyes and sigh before getting back up to stir my oatmeal on
the stove.

Ava raises her eyebrows and with a slight attitude says,
"Well, I didn't feel any type of way about anything or anyone
with something to say about us or me at school. The ones that
make sly digs are well-known haters anyway."

Ava hops up, slides her chair in, walks over, and kisses
my cheek. As she starts toward the stairs, I say to her, "I know
that's right! Wake your brothers for school, okay?"

"Yes ma'am."

As I begin to sort bread for toast, Carlos' office door
creaks open slowly. I hear him but I will not look up. He has to
feel my disappointment. I've lost all respect for him. He's
looking at his phone, I can see it in my peripheral vision. He
looks up. He reluctantly starts toward the kitchen in my
direction. Slowly approaching, he clears his throat to say:
"Good morning, babe."

"Morning," I replied, busying myself by wiping the
countertop. I do not look in his direction. He begins to walk
over to me. He sets his phone down on the countertop. With

tenderness, he touches my right shoulder. I shudder with revulsion. When I wince, he releases my shoulder, dropping his hands to his side. He lifts a brow, "Damn, that's where we're at now? You are still angry?" He stands next to me. I do not look up. I stay silent and busy. "Bae."

"Carlos, this is not the right time. The children will be swarming around in here in about 60 seconds."

He looks up the stairs and says, "Okay, you're right. One question though."

"Alright," as I prepare toast.

"Are we going to end up divorced over this mess?" He says in his quiet voice.

"I don't know, Carlos, but I do know we are in trouble. Serious trouble."

Carlos pushes his eyebrows together to form a wrinkle between his eyes. Narrowing his eyes, he shakes his head and, in disbelief, asks, "Really?"

I glance up at him quickly and notice little David coming down the stairs from his room to greet Carlos and I. "Good morning, buddy!"

As I begin to fix his breakfast plate, Carlos turns away from me to greet him. "Wussup, lil man?"

"Morning, Dad," says David, giving Carlos a high five.

I hear Ava in the shower; Isaiah and Ezekiel start down the stairs toward the kitchen for breakfast. "Hey fellas, good morning."

"Morning, Mom" they reply. Carlos clears his throat with a blank look of disappointment toward the boys as they begin making their plates.

"Oh, sorry," Isaiah says very dryly. "'Sup Dad."

"Morning, Dad," Ezekiel says.

Carlos nods in agreement, walking away from the sink and starting toward them as they join David at the kitchen table. "That's right, y'all betta speak, um hmm. Isaiah, do you have track practice today?"

"No," Isaiah says firm and direct. "I do tomorrow, though."

"What time?" I ask.

"10:00 a.m., but I'd like to get there at 9:45 a.m. if I can. I'm the captain and I want to show leadership." Isaiah takes a scoop of oatmeal and starts to scroll on his smartphone.

"Oh alright, I can drop you off," says Carlos as he gets up and grabs a mug for coffee from the cupboard.

Ezekiel nudges Isaiah and nods to him with his eyebrows raised. "Dad, is it cool if I get a ride with Darren to practice tomorrow?"

"I can take you son, I don't mind." Carlos grabs the coffee pot and begins to pour.

"Speak up, Bro," Ezekiel says quietly to Isaiah.

Carlos glances over and sees the two oldest boys having a quiet disagreement. "What's up, fellas? What's the deal? I peeped y'all just now, be a man and speak ya mind flat out, man." He places the coffee pot back.

"My fault, 'Saiah," Ezekiel starts shaking his head. "Dad, Isaiah does not want to ride in that car you just got the other day."

Carlos raises his eyebrows. "Oh yeah?" he says before he takes a sip of his coffee. "That's how you feel, 'Saiah?"

Isaiah becomes visibly uncomfortable and sets his spoon down into his bowl. "Well Dad, I umm—"

Carlos interrupts. "I know it's not the Range, man, I'm driving this joint temporarily, and it's actually *your* car." He sets his mug on the coaster.

Ezekiel chuckles and says, "For *real?*"

"Yeah, I bought it outright, no payments, it runs good. It's old but not super old, it's a 2004."

Isaiah's body language becomes less tense.

"Can you tell me how long it will be before I get to drive it? I got my permit," Isaiah says eagerly.

"I need to drive it a little while longer." Carlos scoots in closer to the boys to quiet the conversation. "Look, I know that y'all are embarrassed," he starts. I glance over and sigh. I then exit the kitchen down toward the family room. Just far enough, but I can still hear them talking.

Carlos continues: "I saw that shit on the internet and I managed to make some arrangements with the loan agency to get my car back. I figured it would all affect y'all, you know what I'm saying? But you both have been holding it down." His voice was very casual, like he has it all under control. "Now I know it's a lot of drama and a lot of judgment. I saw all of the negative comments that folks who don't even know me are making and speaking on shit that they have no idea about." Carlos is expressive with his hands and says, "I'm going to fix everything, it's a misunderstanding!"

His hands go up in a surrendering motion. Isaiah and Ezekiel are sitting quietly as David starts to the sink to put his spoon and bowl into the basin. "That's all good, Dad, but—"

"But what, 'Saiah?"

"What about Mom?"

"What do you mean?" Carlos leans back into the dining room chair. His eyebrows lift as if he is already prepared to defend himself.

"Is Mom gonna be alright? She hurt her face; she was at Grandma's for three days."

"She's been so quiet," Ezekiel adds.

"Look, y'all," Carlos interrupts with an uneasy smile. "Your mom will be fine, she's strong." He glances in my direction and tries to lower his voice. He quickly looks back at the boys to address his point of view. "When you think about it, I'm the one that is hurt the most! As a man, it looks like I'm not handling business at home! Ya know? I mean, it's rough to see my wife go out like that but, just look at the damage done to my reputation!" The boys look confused as if they can't believe what they are hearing. "Regardless of how anyone feels, she should've reacted differently out in public—"

I interrupt loudly: "Hey fellas, it's already 7:15 a.m., let's get it poppin! Clean up after yourselves and get dressed."

"Yes, ma'am," the boys reply.

Annoyed at Carlos' perspective, I turn the TV on to watch the local news. I steady myself as I set the remote controller down to approach Carlos. I think to myself, under no circumstances am I going to allow him to intimidate or manipulate our crisis into a situation where *he* looks like the victim. *I AM THE VICTIM!* I say in my head. However selfish he's always been, or considered himself, he can't justify his actions, to our children, with no accountability, at my expense! I had to stop him from talking to the boys before he went too far.

"Hey, I don't want them to miss the bus. We should have this conversation another time," I tell him as I am nodding yes.

Carlos gazes in thought at me for a moment, looks away with his eyebrows up and throws his hands up in a surrender motion. "Alright, whatever you want." He then grabs his coffee and starts toward the family room. I go back into the kitchen to load the dishwashing machine as the children thump around upstairs to get ready for school.

The news anchor begins to speak, "Well, good morning, Philadelphia! Thanks for tuning in with your favorite morning team! We have some breaking news to report. It seems that the winner of the Power Millions Jackpot still has not come forward to claim their winnings. Lottery officials say that the winner has 180 days to validate and cash the winning ticket of the drawing date. We have Home Team's own Jeremy West at the Easy Mart where the winning ticket was sold! How ya doing out there, Jeremy, good morning!"

"Can you believe this, bae!? This gas station is literally right around the corner from the house!" Carlos says to me.

"That's crazy," I reply as I finish the dishes.

"One hundred and fifty million dollars! Could you imagine what I could do with that kind of money?" His voice intensifies. "I would get this app off and running. Call Jakka and get the clothing line back up and in business, man." He pauses. "Help Ronnie with the club venture and do some shows." His voice trails off as he begins to daydream. He continues, "I'd get a Lambo, finish my Jordan collection, and we could all go on vacation, buy a condo in New York…"

I roll my eyes and sigh as I shut the dishwasher, trying to get Carlos to snap out of it. "How about pay off some of these loans or put your troubled mother back in rehab," I snarl.

He turns around to look at me and shakes his head. He faces the TV and stands up to stretch as he announces, "I'm gonna head to the shower and go to work." He goes upstairs to prepare for work. I turn the volume down on the TV and turn on the caption so that I can play some music. I select Fireside R&B playlist. First song is Al Green– "Love and Happiness." Word, I love this song. It's a great, soulful song. I check my phone. It is now 7:31 a.m. The children should be done getting dressed by now. Well, that's if they aren't distracted by their phones.

All four of them should be at the bus stop by 7:45 a.m. It's about a 10-minute walk from here. I think I'll walk with them this morning. And besides, I have to get my mind right to be prepared to have this talk that I'm not looking forward to having with Carlos. The children start to make their way in to the foyer and are surprised to see me fully dressed for work with a jacket on to walk them to the bus stop.

Ava, as always, arrives finished first. She sees me dressed and asks, "Are you walking with us, Mom?" She glares excitedly.

"Yes, Munch!" I smile. "Are you shocked?"

"No, I'm glad," as she picks up her book bag. David arrives next, then Ezekiel and Isaiah. "Mom's walking us to the bus stop!" Ava is pleased to announce to her brothers.

"Whoa, really, Mom?" little David asks.

"Yeah! You don't mind, do you? I need the exercise."

"I don't mind, Mom."

"Besides, the sun is out and I want just a little more time with y'all before I start back to work today. Wait, y'all say goodbye to your father, he's in the room getting ready for work." I motion for them to bid farewell.

"Bye, Dad!" they all shout individually.

Carlos cracks the door of the master bedroom to respond to the children, "Alright y'all, peace. Love y'all!"

"Hey! I'm walking with them to the bus stop. I'll be right back, okay?" I yell up to him.

"Alright, be careful," he yells out.

We all walk out the door. I'm last to walk out so I pull up the door to lock it. It's a cool, brisk morning; April in Philly is typically rainy and cool so just cool is good. We begin walking. David puts his hand in mine as he always does. I think to myself, *I have great kids, loving and kind.* I couldn't ask for better kids.

We continue walking when Ava asks a question: "Mom, what time are you going into work today?"

"About 9:00 a.m. I have to go to the hair store first."

"Why so early, Mom? Don't you normally go in at 10:00 a.m.?" Isaiah asks.

"Yeah, I do, I just want to check the condition of Jay's Beauty Salon, really. I left Miss Tina in charge and I don't know if she made sure that everyone did their shop duties. You know what I'm saying? 'Saiah, what time is track practice over tomorrow?"

"About 1:00 p.m."

"Okay cool, I have to tell y'all a secret and you can't tell anyone, not even Dad, okay?"

"Okay Mom," they all reply.

"We have a very special guest coming over tomorrow at about 4:00 p.m. for dinner."

"Who is it?!" Ava asks excitedly.

"It's a surprise! I'm not gonna tell you, Ms. Mouth Almighty!" We all chuckle a bit. Ava struggles with being a bit of a Chatty Patty.

As we approach the bus stop, four children who attend their prep school are already standing there. Ezekiel sees his friend Le'Andre. I know his mother, they live down the street from us. Ezekiel calls out to him: "Yo Andre!"

"Wuz good, Zeek?" he replies as he looks up from his phone. He walks up to Ezekiel and they slap hands. He begins to speak to all of his siblings and then he notices me. "Good morning, Mrs. Jadirah."

As he reaches in for a hug, I hug back. "Good morning, baby, it's good to see you. How's your momma doing?"

"She's doing good. She wants you to know that we are all praying for you."

Isaiah sucks his teeth with annoyance, as he throws his head back and rubs his face. Le'Andre doesn't notice his reaction.

"Well thanks, sweetheart, tell everyone I said hello!"

"Okay, Mrs. Jay."

"Bye everyone, have a great Friday, be leaders…"

"Not followers!" say Ava and David.

The other two wave goodbye as I start my journey back home. I finally take my phone off airplane mode. When I'm with my children I do not do business or hold long conversations on the phone. I notice that I have six missed calls: two from my mother, one from Tina, one from my first client Mrs. Wheeler, and two from Nisa. I will call Nisa back. I dial, she picks up right away after two rings. She had to see it was me.

"Sis!?" Nisa answers.

"Hey sis!" I say.

"Oh my goodness, how are you?"

"I'm good, I feel blessed. I'm walking right now."

"Where to?"

"Back home, I walked the babies to the bus stop this morning. Where are you?"

"I'm in England right now; we're coming straight to the Philly airport."

"I'm so excited!"

"Don't tell anyone I'm coming, I do not want to talk about the reality show, Jak's reunion concert, NOTHING! You are my Sis, I'm coming for you and to check on my godbabies. Don't tell nobody, not even Fuck Boy!"

"Nisa, please stop calling him that."

"It's true!! How could he let that shit happen to you?" She quiets her voice, "He let you go out like that in front of your business. It was his car, correct? Did he even consider how you've been feeling?"

"Yep, it was his car."

"Did you get yours out of the mechanic shop with what I sent?"

"Yes, that very same day, Sis. I… don't want to talk about this shit right now. How was Tokyo? How is business? What's Jakka been up to? How are the kids?" I ask as I continue walking home.

"All is well, I'm glad to be coming back home, for real. Life is hectic right now with all of these deadlines." Nisa lowers her voice, "I have to tell you, Jay, Jakka sent me that clip. He DM'd it to me and I cried. I wanna fight this nigga Carlos! You would NEVER let something like that happen to *him*!"

"Nisa…"

"You know… that I'm right."

"We will talk when you get here; you already know I hate talking on the phone, Nisa."

"Hold on, Sis—*Yeah, yes no problem! I love you too!*" Nisa says to fans. "Sorry Sis, taking selfies with fans at the airport. I gotta go, we are about to board the G4. I love you and I am on my way!"

"Peace, Sis, be careful. Love you!"

"Peace, love you, too!"

By the time I end the call with my sister friend Nisa, I look up and I'm getting closer to my front yard. I take a deep breath before slowly approaching the front door. I exhale. I feel overwhelmed already.

I sigh, trying to mentally prepare myself for all of Carlos' bullshit. He blames me for anything that goes wrong in this relationship. I need a moment. I step onto the front porch. I see him looking out the window. I once again try to brace myself for whatever comes of this conversation that I have been avoiding.

Carlos unlocks and opens the door. I walk in. As he shuts the front door, I sigh heavily and I close my eyes for a moment.

"How was the walk?" Carlos asks.

"It was fine, they enjoyed it," I said.

"Okay, okay, can we sit in the family room, just real quick?"

"Yeah, of course, real quick, I know that you want to get to work so…"

"Okay. I have a plan that I think will work out."

I cross my legs at the knees, rest my elbow on the arm of the couch and I bring my hand up and rest my face and chin upon my left hand. I'm getting ready to hear a whole bunch of talk; he loves to hear himself talk.

Carlos continues: "I called the loan company and they said that we will need $4,200 to get the Range back. The only problem is that we don't have enough, I checked the kids' college account and it's not enough in there to cover it. My paycheck is not enough with what I had in cash but I noticed that you got your BMW out the shop the day of 'The Incident' and I just want to know if you are hiding… any money from me? 'Cause look, Bae, the repairs on that Beemer was nearly $3,000! I know this because I spoke to the mechanic. You knew I was behind on the mortgage and I was gonna get the car payments caught up once we got the income tax check! And… I didn't know they were gonna blow down on you like that. My plan was to take care of everything that was behind and we wouldn't be behind on payment… if you just fill those other two chairs at Jay's Beauty Salon! I mean, damn! Work smarter, not harder, Babe. You know I don't want you killing yourself working 14-hour days. We gotta figure out how to make more money. I am going to fine-tune this app that Ronnie and I are working on. It's gonna be hot! We're almost finished working on the details. I won't stand for anything less than excellence."

I remain silent, I glance at my phone to see what time it is. It's 8:14 a.m.

"What?" Carlos asks.

"Hmmm?" I ponder as I raise my eyebrows.

"You get a message or something?"

"Just checking the time, it's 8:14 but go ahead."

"Well, that was pretty much it. You have to know that I'm working hard, Babe, I'm putting a plan together to put us back on top. This all has been a test, I just know it."

I sit up straight, clear my throat and ask him very calmly: "May I respond?"

"Of course," Carlos replies as he moves a pillow from his side.

Before I respond to everything he has said, I grab my purse and keys and place them right beside me. Then I grab my laptop bag and place it on the ground near my foot. Carlos looks confused but he should not be confused. When we have to talk like this, things typically take a turn for the worse and nothing gets solved. I begin, very calmly and slowly:

"So, this… plan works good for you?"

Carlos nods yes.

"It does not work for me—and I'll tell you why. Carlos, you do not like to make payments on ANYTHING! Purchasing that Range was a mistake to begin with because of the interest rate and your credit score. We couldn't bring a big downpayment in because we had spent the money we had saved for the closing costs and downpayment for the house. Our budget was stretched too thin! Going to get that car *back* is a huge mistake. Now as far as the college account is concerned, I've known for some time what the balance is—"

Carlos interrupts: "Imma fix that, too! It's on the way!"

"Hold on, let me finish, I didn't cut *you* off."

He nods in agreement.

"Okay, their college account was established by their godparents. It should have never been touched, period!" Carlos remains silent. "As far as the BMW is concerned, I borrowed the money from Nisa that very same day of the repossession —"

Carlo interrupts: "Bae, c'mon please say 'Incident.'"

"I'll call it what it is, Carlos. Your Range Rover was repossessed in front of *my* beauty salon for nonpayment."

Carlos is clearly annoyed. "So, anyway, you got hooked up with some dough and didn't tell me? How much did she send you?" he asks, trying to change the subject.

"As I said, she loaned me the $2,900 for repairs and not a penny more. That's nothing for her and Jakka. So back to what I was saying. I was not aware that you had gotten behind on the mortgage. I was under the impression that you would take care of your truck payment with the income tax money, and now that you bought this used truck, you should just drive that since there aren't any payments on it. That way you can tell the loan company to keep the Range! We never could afford it anyway! I am, however, hurt that you could not call me up to communicate with me that I was going to be *humiliated* in front of my business. If that's not bad enough, the shit goes viral on the internet. Can you understand how difficult things have been for me? I had to go and pick our children up from that uppity prep school in a yellow cab!?!"

The pain came at the thought of the whole ordeal. My voice begins to crack from the raw emotion. I stand up. I am no longer calm, I'm furious and feel rage. I continue: "I had blood and scrapes on my face because I tripped and fell trying to chase down and stop the fucking repo man! The whole goddamn neighborhood was watching me panic and everyone was looking. I was HUMILIATED! You couldn't keep up the payments and had me dropping you off at work. Me picking up the kids! And you couldn't tell me that the man was coming to get the car?! You don't have the money to make the payments because of your foolhardy business schemes—"

Carlos interrupts: "Nah, hold it, Jay!"

"No, Los, you hold it one muthafuckin minute! I have been trying to wait on you to get it together and not be so selfish. You have a family! You are supposed to be a protector and provider. I have been patient. I stuck with you when you cheated, I stayed when you lost your job and I had to work two. Hell, I stayed with you through two evictions too, and through all of the bullshit your mother throws this way and I'm tired! You keep talking about this app. What about all' the other projects that we've started together? The short film, the online magazine—"

Carlos interrupts again: "That shit ain't gonna make no real money, creating this app will make us millionaires. I know that you don't believe in it but I do, shit! You need to talk to Nisa, so she can invest!"

I fall silent. Clearly frustrated, I put my hands on my face and rub downward in one stroke. He will not let me finish my point because he keeps interrupting me. So I sit silently, trying to tune him out. By now he's pacing and ranting about what he could have been. I don't really know. I'm sitting there patiently, waiting, hoping to hear an apology.

I am so miserable in this moment. It sounds like he's brushing the worst thing to ever happen to me to the side. Okay, now it sounds like he's worried about his damaged reputation of being a good man that can hold his family down. *Okay, where is my phone*, I say to myself as Carlos' rant continues. I expected all of this, I did, but now I'm done. Here's my phone. I glance at the time and say aloud during his rant, "It's 8:31, you and I should be getting to work!" Absolutely nothing had been accomplished here.

"Alright, whatever!" he says in a moody way.

"We're gonna work through all this shit later tonight when I get off." I say, annoyed at him.

"Have a good day at work today, Jadirah," Carlos says in a tongue-in-cheek manner as I gather my things and stand up, walking toward the front door. I glance back at him quickly as I shake my head in disbelief.

Shaking off my mood on my way to the car, I feel drained. Not even triggered or saddened, just drained. I hop into my car and I pause, realizing he never mentioned an apology. Sure, he texted it to me the day of the incident, but he can't bring himself to say it? What a jackass! I didn't even get to finish my point! I have to admit, I no longer have respect for my husband. Time to get on with my day.

TWO

What's the 411?

In my car I feel safe. I spend a lot of time in my car, running errands for the family and my business. I am comfortable. With serious effort, I manage to pull my emotions back in and force them to settle. My eyes are closed. I am a woman, a business owner, and a mother with responsibilities and ambitions.

"Shake it out, Jadirah," I say to myself in an authoritative voice. I start up my silver 2001 BMW 3-Series and select my music. Yes, Jagged Edge, Dru Hill and Faith Evans mix is on. I shift to drive and peel off to the supply store first.

As I ride, I can't help but wonder about Carlos. I wonder if he even knows how blessed he is. A woman—a loyal woman—hardworking, successful, with four beautiful children who are smart, respectful and naturally kind-hearted. Maybe if he knew what he has, he could learn to appreciate this family that we've built. However, I have just decided to give up hope. All this time I'd hoped to teach him or guide though example. This is a feeling that I've never experienced before. I can tell that I no longer give a fuck.

I'm not a young girl caught up in fairytales anymore. I am not weak or ashamed. Ashamed of believing that I could change my husband. I will not be used, ignored and I will no longer find passivity easier than using straight words with Carlos. I am exhausted and replete with regrets.

"I have work to do," I murmur to myself, as Sisqo belts out "Beauty is her name" on my stereo system. I begin to sing along to take my mind off of things: " 'Cause my eyes have seen the glory, in the coming of your smile, so I swear if you ever come around again, please stay for a while."

As I pull up to the hair supply store parking lot, I hear my phone as if I have just received a text message. I don't look because I'm searching for a parking spot. I park and check my phone. The text message is from Mrs. Wheeler and says: "Good morning Jadirah. Just checking in to see if we are still on for 10:00 a.m. this morning."

I reply: "Morning! Yes, I'll see you then."

She responds by texting "Thank you."

At that very moment, Carlos' text: "Hey bae, look, I love you so much and I want to resolve any issues between us immediately. Okay? Also could you possibly check with Nisa about loaning me $5,000 to get my truck back? This lil used truck is not for me. It's Isaiah's whip, straight up. I don't want my credit report getting messed up again. I would be grateful." I look up from my phone, exasperated. I shake my head in disbelief. This man clearly has his head up his ass and is committed to ignoring all of our marital and trust issues!

Unbothered, I sigh. I do not reply and toss my cell into my bag. Gather myself and head into the store. I enter the store and look around quickly. I think to myself, *Good, I'm the only customer in here.*

The clerk greets me: "Good morning!"

"Good morning! How ya doin?"

"Just fine, let me know if you need help finding anything."

"Okay, thanks."

She smiles and walks away. I pull out my list. Yes, I still make a list on notebook paper. Okay. Rubber bands, vinyl gloves, bobby pins, wide wrap strips and 90% alcohol. Alright, let me get to it. It's 9:05 a.m. already. I purchase my items and thank the clerk as I start on my way to work. Once I arrive at work, I park around back so that the customers can have access to the closest parking spaces and entrance to Jay's Beauty Salon. It's not a big salon, more of a boutique salon with only four of us working here. I love the setup. I've worked in full-service large salons and it is not my forte to manage all those personalities at once and do great work!

In Jay's Beauty Salon, there's Tina, my lead stylist on duty to manage things when I'm away. She's an amazing and talented stylist but she throws shade like a girl from those reality TV shows! She's friends with most of her clientele and she can code switch into "Professional Katina" when she has new clients.

There's Lelah, my first cousin, the master aesthetician. She's part-time and is always booked. She's a full-time nurse with two very busy kids; they must be involved in every activity known to man! She has a professional, pleasant disposition. We grew up together and grew apart when she went away to college and I moved to New York for work. She's hyper-vigilant about her personal life. She literally keeps a closed position when it comes to her personal life. She's been that way ever since she lost her brother. He was in the streets and was murdered. The whole family was devastated. She hasn't been the same since. Sometimes I see her crying in the car on her lunch break. Bless her heart.

Lastly, we have Ja'Nay. Lord have MERCY, our gifted and creative nail technician. What an amazing talent she is. Although she's only twenty-two, she's one of the coldest nail artists I've ever seen. But, I'm sad to say that she is unprofessional, loud, lazy, entitled, spoiled, disrespectful, and always late! A very pretty girl with her 18-inch jet-black silk-press weave parted straight down the middle with the lace frontal and perfectly laid baby hairs. Her brows micro-bladed to perfection and those mink eyelashes are simply to die for. The Bad Bitch. Every shop has one. She wears the Bad Bitch uniform unlike any other.

That's the way it is. They all show respect to me because I'm the veteran in this business and because they know my reputation as a successful industry stylist. I've had six publications, five fashion weeks, twelve plays and countless Hip Hop and R&B music videos, just to name a few. I had it going on in the late '90s, early 2000's and I'm grateful for those experiences.

As I approach the front door of my beauty salon, I notice flowers, gift bags that have candles in jars and balloons that read "Get well soon." I curl my lips into a slight smile as I speed up the pace to take all of the gifts into the shop. I'm uncomfortable, but grateful. I quickly unlock the door, set my bags down and shut the alarm off. Turn on the lights and rush outside to grab what appears to be a site where somebody was gunned down in the 'hood! I am truly grateful for all the love, but I can't stand all this attention.

I get everything settled and turn to my work station. I gasp, then grin; the girls have decorated my station with a Happy Birthday banner and balloons. My birthday was April 1st. My station looks so nice. *I'm* the one to decorate workstations! "Oh my goodness, red roses!" I say, standing there admiring the work that the ladies put into all of this. I pull out my cell to check the time, it's 9:45 a.m. I'd better get a move on, my first client will be here shortly. I get my music going. I need to ease into this day, expect the unexpected, no drama. Let's see, *ahh!* Robert Glasper and a little John Coltrane afterward.

I do a once-over on the restrooms and I check the floors. *Ha*, they cleaned and mopped! I am pleased with the condition of my salon. The ladies have passed my brief inspection. Time to get to work.

Doorbell rings, I buzz Mrs. Wheeler in. She opens the door and says, "Good morning, Mrs. Jadirah!"

"Good morning, Mrs. Wheeler! How have you been?" I reply.

"I've been doin' good, honey." Her eyes dance over to my work station, "Oh, happy birthday!"

"Thank you!"

"How old are you, sweetheart?"

"41 years old."

"Oh, sugar, you're still a young one," she chuckles. "Wait till you're 68 like me!"

"Well, you are doing great, Mrs. Wheeler. What did you want to have done today?"

"Just a wash and roller set, sugar," she says as she sits down at the shampoo bowl, placing her purse in her lap. We make small talk through the shampoo and condition. I towel dry her freshly-shampooed tresses and we head over to the styling chair. I wet-set her hair on medium-sized rollers and place her under the pre-heated dryer. Mrs. Wheeler begins to ask me a few questions:

"So Mrs. Jadirah, what are you all doing for your birthday?

"Oh, I don't know, maybe my husband has something planned," I respond as I start to wipe down my chair.

"Do you think he has planned a surprise party?" she says very smoothly.

"I don't think so."

"I hope not, baby, the word at my church is that," she widens her eyes, "you hate surprises!" I stop wiping my chair and look directly at her. "I know I can't stand surprises, honey!"

"Most people hate surprises," I smile and continue to wipe down my chair.

"Maybe he should take you on a cruise or you suggest some nice jewelry. You work so hard, honey, you deserve a very nice birthday."

I stop cleaning. "Mrs. Wheeler, will you excuse me? I need to grab something out of the break room."

She nods yes. She smiles a little as she leans over to grab a magazine off of the side table. I get to the break room and I pause. I think to myself: was it too soon to come back to work? I'm the word on the street? Did Mrs. Wheeler just try and throw some nice shade? I thought the drama had died down by now! I quickly gathered myself and walked back out into the salon.

"Mrs. Wheeler would you like some water?" I ask.

"No thank you, I'm fine, baby," she replied. I sit down at the desk and I plug my laptop to the charger. As I look over my schedule, I realize I'm booked for the day. I sigh in gratitude for the moment, at this moment, it is calm and peaceful. The rest of the day will be so busy.

I think everyone is getting their hair done for the comedy show this weekend. Cheryl Underwood is doing her standup show and she is hilarious. My next client isn't until 11:30 a.m., so I have time to chill and I'll browse the web for a little while. I remind myself to stay off social media.

Time passes, it is now 10:50 a.m. and the doorbell rings. I look out and it's an unfamiliar face. I buzz her in. She enters. "Good morning, what can I do for you?" I ask.

"Hi, I have an appointment with Ja'Nay," she replies.

"Okay, what's your name?"

"Day'Jah."

"Okay, what time is your appointment?"

"It's for 11 a.m., but I've never been here before so I wanted to get here early, to give myself time."

"I understand, you can hang your jacket here," I point to the closet. "The waiting area is right here," I point to the lobby space. "Make yourself at home."

"Okay, thanks." She sits down and begins texting.

Mrs. Wheeler's dryer shuts off and I check to see if her hair has dried thoroughly.

"Alright, Mrs. Wheeler, all set, we can move on over to the first chair," I say in my friendly folksy voice. As I begin to remove the rollers, Mrs. Wheeler reminds me to put a "lil" oil on her scalp and not to comb her curls out. "Ok, all set!" I say as I remove the comb and undo the cape.

"Thank you, sweetheart," she says, as she hands me a check and a folded up piece of paper. "I'm going to get going." She stands and grabs her purse. Opens her arms for a hug, I hug. "Baby, you're tougher than you look, thank the Lord."

"Thank you so much," I say, releasing my hug.

"Thank *you* so much," she says, releasing the hug. "You ladies have a good one."

"Okay thanks!"

"Bye," Day'Jah says.

I unfold the little piece of paper and it reads: "God is our refuge and strength, an ever-present help in trouble. Psalm 46:1-3." I smile, and fold the paper back up and place it in my bag. I grab my phone to check the time, it is 11:15 a.m. I then turn to Ja'Nay's client and ask:

"So, has she texted you?"

"Yeah, she says she's on the way."

"Okay." I take a seat to text Ja'Nay about her client. She texts right back and tells me she's running behind, and I begin to feel a faint drop of sympathy for this young lady. She probably saw her work on the Gram. I just don't understand the work ethic of Ja'Nay's generation. Time is money!

The doorbell rings, I hope it's Ja'Nay. Nope, it's Tina and she's holding cupcakes! *Aww!* I open the door for her because I can clearly see that her hands are full.

"Hey girl!" I say to her.

"Hey, Jay! Happy belated! These are for you and I bought enough for all of the customers, too!" I take the first box and she says, "Lemme grab the other stuff, Imma be right back."

I begin to set the baked goods down. When I turn to the door, my next client is approaching and I rush to open the door because I see Tina and Ja'Nay right behind her.

"Good morning!" all the ladies greet me with delight.

"Welcome back, Mrs. Jay, how are you feeling?" asks Ja'Nay.

"Couldn't be better, I feel refreshed! This is exciting, Tina, I hope you didn't go through too much trouble, sis."

"No problem at all; we all pitched in. We wanted you to enjoy your first day back. We didn't want no drama, all love!"

"I know that's right," my client Marshay chimes in.

I take Marshay to the shampoo bowl to get started, as I carefully eavesdrop on Ja'Nay and Day'Jah's conversation. Everything seems calm. I didn't hear Ja'Nay apologize for being late, though. Noted, stored in my database. The next four hours of the business day is typical shop talk, gossip and talk of current events in news, politics, and the staff making prom appointments. I'm pleased at how peaceful the energy has been. Everyone's clients have been so friendly and kind in wishing me a happy birthday.

I check the time and I notice that the children will be getting out of school in about 45 minutes. My mother will be picking them up from school today. She agreed to help out for a while until our family issues become stable. I shoot her a text to remind her about the parent pick-up line. I send the text and take a sip of my alkaline water. I look and see Lelah approaching the door; she's fumbling her keys and holding the most beautiful arrangement of white roses that I've ever seen. She unlocks the door and steps in.

"Good morning, ladies," she says, smiling in her ladylike sweetheart voice. The ladies reply. She approaches me. "Hey cuz, these are for you. Happy Birthday, let me know if you need anything." She rushes through the words. Gives me a quick hug and speed-walks to her booth.

"Thank you so much! They're beautiful!" The ladies agree aloud and I hear gasps.

Tina has a question while she's working on a sew-in weave: "Jay!"

"Wassup?" I respond.

"Is the Friday crew coming in tonight?"

"Yep! All five."

"Okay, is Jena bringing wine? Cause a sistah could use a little Vino!" Tina laughs.

"Absolutely, sis. I could use a little help if you don't have any clients scheduled." Phone rings, its Mom. "Hey Mom!"

"Hey sweetheart, I'm on the way," Mom says.

"Okay, you're going to swing by the shop first, right?"

"Yes! Then we're gonna pick up a couple of pies from Lorenzo and Sons."

"Oooh, that sounds good! They'll love that."

"Did you want anything, baby? I can stop and grab whatever you need."

"I'm good, Mom."

"How has the first day back been?"

"It's been cool, I might have to have a sidebar convo with Ja'Nay though in a bit. She was super late for her first client this morning."

"Oh lord, I tried to tell you about that one, honey, I knew she was a pistol."

"Yeah, did Daddy go to Jumu'ah prayer today?"

"Yes, he should be back home by now. I'll call him in a bit."

"Okay, Mom, lemme let you go and I'll see you soon."

"Okay, sweetheart, love you!"

"Love ya back!" We end the call.

I'm hot-curling one of my favorite clients, Shay, when Tina says, "Oh my goodness!" She doesn't realize how loud she is because almost everyone in the salon looks up and over at her. "Oops, I'm sorry ladies!" she's shaking her head at the cellphone with a smirk on her face and then shows her client in her styling chair. I'm kinda curious and maybe a little nervous because now they're making quiet slick remarks about the video on social media. I'm thinking some idiot has remixed and put music to my very public, embarrassing situation from last week. I glance over at Tina. She sees me and says, "Sis, take a look at this heffa." She walks over and shows me and Shay the short clip.

Shay says, "Who is that? Is that ol' girl from 106?"

Tina says, "Yes, but peep out her squats though! I can't stand these workout chicks on the 'Gram!"

"I can't stand them either, but you gotta admit her body is bangin' though!" Shay says, looking at the phone.

I jump in to throw some shady humor to show Tina that I really am okay. "Hyper bitch!" I murmured. "She needs to sit down before she put her back out!"

Tina and Shay laugh. Tina loves shade! I continue on with Shay's appointment until she is finished. We chat as I check her out and schedule her next appointment.

I get a call, it's an unknown number. Hmmm, I think I'll let that one go to voicemail. "Ok, Shay, I'll see ya in two weeks."

"Ok, have a good one, Jay!" We hug and say bye.

Phone rings again from the unknown caller. I decide to answer the call this time. "This is Jadirah, may I help you?"

"Hi, this is Day'Jah from this morning."

"Yes, hi there."

"Yeah, so I just wanted to make a complaint. Not against your shop, you have a really nice shop but I just feel like Ja'Nay should have given me a gift certificate or a discount for being so late today. She didn't even apologize and I'm sorry but a real one like me won't stand for this type of behavior. I like my nails, but I did not like my experience though."

"Well, I'm sorry about that, Day'Jah, I will speak to her immediately about this. You have a good day."

I hang up and check the time. I have about ten minutes before my next client. Good, just enough time to have a lil chat with our tardy but talented nail tech. As I walk to her station I quickly notice that her client has just been placed in the nail drying light. Good! What I need to say will only take five minutes anyway.

"Ja'Nay, do you have a minute?"

"Yeah, it's cool, what's up?" She places her phone down, props her elbow up onto her work station and rests her chin in the palm of her hand.

I sigh. I'm frustrated. I say "In private? In the break room."

"Ooh okay, Mrs. Jay."

We go to the break room and I shut the door. I begin, "Ja'Nay, your client called me to complain about her service today, your first client…."

Ja'Nay interrupts: "Well, before you get started, I just wanna say that I had text her and told her I was gonna be late so…"

"That's the thing, sis, you have to learn to be on time for your customers. You will lose business and your reputation will suffer!"

Her body language is closed and she becomes defensive. "How are you gonna talk to me about my reputation!? I'm the coldest nail stylist in Philly! Bitches should be thanking their lucky stars that they could even get an appointment with me."

"Ja'Nay, that is beside the point. I've seen the best struggle to keep their clientele because they were unprofessional and arrogant! You have to do better if you want to continue on in this business! And when the word gets out that there is someone out there that is just as good as you, just as creative but professional with a pleasant disposition, except they are hungry, starving and can't wait to work? Your rep will struggle and you will lose your clientele."

"Mrs. Jay, no disrespect but you got some nerve comin' at me about reputation nonsense, when your shit is messy and all over the internet. Are you serious? You was the coldest stylist all over the east coast, all those music videos and fashion shows. You are friends with Jakka and Nisa Hyatt. All of your success and you can't even pay a car note? Please, you're washed."

"Ja'Nay, watch it! You are so disrespectful and I will not tolerate it. You will call your client and apologize and you will offer her a free polish change as a peace offering! Am I making myself clear?" She rolls her eyes and sucks her teeth. I look at her over the top of my glasses and use my firm voice tone, "Ja'Nay, are we clear?"

"Yeah, yeah alright. Are we done? I gotta get back to my customer, don't wanna be unprofessional," she murmured.

"Go ahead, we're done." I allow Ja'Nay to walk ahead of me back out onto the salon floor. I had no idea how she felt about me, but now I know. I know that I'm going to be thinking about the things that she said later.

About thirty minutes pass when my mother arrives with my children. She has a key so she opens the door. The children are waving at me through the window. The door opens and the first one to greet me is little Ava. "Hey, Mommy!"

"Hi, sweetheart, say hello to the ladies."

"Hi everyone," she says with a smile and a wave.

The ladies reply with smiles as some of the long-time customers begin to ask them about their grades and they comment on how tall they've gotten. They all give me a hug one by one. My mother gets the last hug. She hugs tight and rocks from side to side slightly, as she whispers, "How are you feeling, baby?"

"I'm doing good, Mom."

"Hi there, Mrs. Diane!" Tina greets my mother.

"Katina!" Mom reaches for a hug. They embrace. Laughter from them both.

"Mrs. Diane, you hug just like my Big Ma! I love it," she chuckles.

"Honey, that's the only way I know how to hug!" Mom says, smiling.

Mom and I begin a little small talk for a while when she notices that Ja'Nay's client is on her cell phone using street language and curse words. Lelah comes out of her work room and very quickly shoots me a look that reads, "HANDLE IT PLEASE."

As I excuse myself from my Mom she says, "No problem, baby, you're the boss!" As I approach the rude, classless client, Ja'Nay makes eye contact with me and shakes her head, *no*. I disregard.

This client is a piece of work. "Yeah girl, fuck that! I wouldn't put up with that shit, I woulda been put that nigga out if he can't even keep a job!" She is saying all of this on her phone as if she thinks the salon thinks that it's cute or funny.

I tap her on the shoulder: "Excuse me."

"Yeah," she replies as if I'm bothering her.

I lower my voice in an attempt to not shame her. "We don't allow cursing in here, you are welcome to speak on your phone outside."

"Tamika lemme call you back, they trippin up here at Jay's Beauty Salon," she says angrily. She ends the call and looks me up and down as Ja'Nay continues to work on her full set. "Now is that better for you, Miss Sadity?"

"Much better, actually!" says my mother sitting at the chair next to my work station. "From Mama Sadity."

The entire salon erupts in laughter. The client turns forward in her chair toward Ja'Nay to finish her service as I say thank you to her. I turn to walk away and I hear Ja'Nay mumble, "I'm so sorry, they be trippin."

The client then says, "Why they so bougie up in here?"

I let it slide. I'm tired of Ja'Nay today. My mother and my children are done with their short visit and she reminds me that I have been summoned by my grandmother to drop off grocery items for tomorrow. She affectionately calls her mother in-law "Sister Faye."

"C'mon babes, say bye to your mom," she says with a faint smile. The children all come over to give me a quick hug each and a murmur of "Love you, Mom."

The day continues on as I prepare for the Friday crew to come in. The Friday crew consists of five women who I've been styling for the past ten years. They are accomplished, proud, smart black women who have become sister-friends because their appointments were scheduled around the same time of day, after 5:00 p.m. Sometimes, they'll bring new snacks, wine, or new foods that they've discovered at new restaurants. We share our ups and downs, what's new and, of course, we gossip. It's a no-judgment zone. Safety.

I'm wiping down my styling mirror when I notice Ja'Nay and Tina having a conversation, and they are whispering. I have a feeling Ja'Nay isn't over me confronting her client about using street language in my salon.

Tina speaks up, "Hey Jay, we'll be right back," she says to me as she starts toward the door with Ja'Nay. Ja'Nay doesn't look up.

"Okay," I reply. They are standing outside right next to the side window and today it's cracked open a bit. I can hear their conversation. I hear Tina say, "You should not approach it like that, Sis. You need to give a two-week notice. She's been through enough as it is!"

"What does that have to do with me, Tina? I'm not going to continue to work for no stuck-up, broke bitch that wanna act like she's some type of boss runnin shit! No, uh uh, I'm outta here."

"Well, technically you can't leave or she could take you to court for the balance. If you pay her two weeks and then leave, then that would be acceptable. Just look it up in your contract."

Turning away from Tina, Ja'Nay rolls her eyes and gives a frustrated exhale. "I'm just going to give a two-week notice then, fine!"

They continue to chat as I move away from the window. I am not surprised by Ja'Nay at all. I don't even care that she wants to go. It might be better for the salon anyway. Her energy is negative and her clientele is toxic. Ja'Nay doesn't respect the shop, perhaps she never had.

I go into the dispensary to grab a bottle of water and to have a seat for a minute or two. Lela comes in to rinse off some metal implements, and as I greet her, she asks how I'm doing. I reply with "It's all good!" I'm easy going, trying to mentally prepare myself for Ja'Nay's resignation.

As Lela leaves out of the dispensary, Ja'Nay walks in. "Hey," I say as I sip my water.

"Sup," she says as she opens the mini fridge to grab her juice. She opens her juice to take a sip. "Ms. Jay," she begins "I am just going to come right out and say it…"

"Go ahead, Ja'Nay, I'll understand."

"…I just wanted to tell you face-to-face that I need to put my two-week notice in today."

I nod, I expected this.

She continues, "I just feel like it's time for me to move on and I know Jay's Beauty Salon contract says that I'm supposed to hand in a resignation letter—"

"No it's fine!" I interrupt. "It's okay, movement is life."

She raises her eyebrows as if she's surprised at my reaction. She nods and then takes a sip of her juice.

"Yeah, so no worries about that letter. It's not important and we are not in the year 1985." I smile to break the ice and she chuckles a bit. I can tell that she is relieved that I played cool. She's talented, but her clientele does not fit in well at my salon. She's unprofessional and, well, I'm not exactly depressed or angry that she feels the need to move on.

We walk out onto the salon floor. Tina is just coming to get me to let me know that Jena is here for her appointment. I'm excited, I've been texting Jena all week. She is my cousin but also one of my best clients and part of the Friday crew.

I love the Friday crew. I don't go out so these ladies bring the party to me. I look forward to Friday nights with these ladies. I have to admit, Friday nights are the best because they remind me of myself before I got married and had children.

Back 2 Love

"Hey Sis! Happy Belated!" Jena smiles at me, giving a sweeping look as if to say, "are you okay?" She has a grin and open arms starting toward me for an embrace.

I laugh, "Good to see ya, sistah cousin!"

"Hey girl, we are going to turn up tonight! The ladies are on the way, I have the wine, Pillar and Nakia are bringing the food, Pamela and Kayla are bringin' the dessert!"

Tina hears Jena and says, "Girl, I'm stayin' to kick it with y'all tonight!"

"Well, come on, Tina, the more the merrier!"

"What style did you want to have done tonight, sis?" I ask Jena.

"Just flat-ironed, I washed it this morning, and have leave-in conditioner on it, it's probably still damp."

"No problem, I'll blow-dry it." We start toward my chair and Cheryl and Pamela are starting towards the door. I buzz them in. "Hey girl!"

"What's good, birthday girl?"

"Hey ladies!" I smile as I hug them both. "What have y'all been up to?"

"Nothin, same old same for me," Cheryl says.

"I got some news, but imma share when the rest of the crew gets here!"

"Okay, Pammy, that's cool," I say as they both head toward the community table to set the goodies and drinks up. As I'm chatting with Jena, Pillar, Nakia and Kayla show up. I buzz them in.

"Ladies! It's on and poppin!" Nakia announces as she and the rest of the ladies enter and greet one another.

"I stocked up on the vino! I hope somebody brought some pretzels or Chex mix!" Jena announces with a short laugh.

"I brought the snacks for that!" Pillar giggles out.

As the small talk continues and the ladies simmer down a bit, I invite Tina's clients to make a plate and pour a drink. I knew that being together on Friday night would boost my morale. We carry on and on until all of the clients have gone for the night. Tina stays behind after Ja'Nay and Lelah take off.

I needed this, I needed the normalcy of it. Even if it was just for a few hours.

Kayla walks over to my work station and sets a cup on my station beside me. Smiling. "Sis, what is this?"

I lift the cup and smell the drink to see if there's alcohol in it. "It's non-alcoholic, GMO free, champagne!" I reply.

"Girl! Yeah right, where can you find such a thing?" Nakia blurts out.

The ladies begin to clamor with laughter and I decide to make a decision. "Ladies, now you know I don't drink but it's been a rough week and I could use a time out! Just this once, and I'll be back on my square tomorrow. So, fuck it!" I point to Pillar, "Bartender! Pour out a lil liquor!"

The ladies begin to laugh and clap with delight at my decision to turn up with them. I go to my phone to cue up "Pour Out A Little Liquor," by Tupac. The first few notes spark the ladies up and we all begin to two-step and groove. Yeah, this is the jam. I'm sipping my champagne and living in the joy and spontaneity of the moment. We dance and rap the entire song. When the song ends we settle down because Sade's song "Like A Tattoo" comes on. That song makes you mellow out. We shift gears.

Cheryl has a question. "Jadirah, how are you, girl?"

"I'm doing good now that I got a buzz going on!"

Cheryl puts her snack plate on the side table and reaches for my left hand and grabs it. She asks again, making eye contact. "Jay, how are you doing, sis?"

I realize what she is really asking me. I look around at the other ladies as the quiet settles over the shop. I don't feel ashamed to talk about "The Incident." I feel comfortable enough in this space, with these women, to open up.

I set my cup down onto my station. The ladies quietly take a seat as I look up at the ceiling to carefully select my words to describe how I have been feeling. "I feel... embarrassed." I nod. "It felt like a really horrible nightmare. I feel humiliated, sis."

"Why didn't you tell us that you all were struggling, sis? You know we would have helped y'all? That shit went viral on the internet!" Jena said.

"Carlos told me that we were behind on the payment. He didn't say anything about us being in danger of a repossession! I woulda paid that. I didn't know! It was *his* car, not mine. My shit is paid off. I drove his car to work that day because my car was being serviced. I got the money and got my car from the mechanic that night." I shake my head and laugh. "Do you know what else? I had to call a cab to go and pick up the children from school. I was pissed!"

Tina chimes in, "Jay, you could've called me, I would've gone to get the babies."

"No. I wanted to do it. I was actually on my way to get them when I heard the car alarm go off from the repo man breaking into the car and that's what made me run outside! I thought someone was breaking into the car!"

"We saw you running on the video. Bitch, you looked like Flo-Jo out this piece!" Cheryl jokes and lightens the mood. The whole room erupts in laughter.

"And when you fell… I was like, aww damn, that shit bout ta hurt!" Nakia adds.

"You see my face is healing up though." I turn to the mirror to look. "I didn't even realize that I was bleeding from my face because my adrenaline was moving. The cab driver gave me a Kleenex like, 'Oh no miss, did you get into a fight?' I was all fucked up, y'all."

"No way, you are better than me, sis, I would have destroyed everything in sight. And I love Carlos and everything but niggas ain't shit. Do he even know the caliber of a woman you are?" Nakia exclaims.

"I was pissed! I was livid!"

We all laughed a bit. Pamela, the one of us who has maintained her voice of being the scholar of the group asks, "But how do you feel now? Today? We all get how you felt the day it happened, it was a tragedy. How are you today, beloved?"

I take a deep breath and close my eyes for a moment. I sigh and I pause a moment because I know exactly what I need to say for them to "get it:"

"You know, I feel…" I sit up in my chair and straighten my posture. "Ok, check this out. You ride through the hood and you see an eviction pile on the curb right? You look over and see a $5,000 Chanel jacket with the trash and broken furniture all around. It's dirt everywhere, a cat might have pissed on the eviction pile, but it's still a Chanel tweed jacket! Limited edition! Rare! And whomever was in that house…" I pause, "had no idea about the value of that jacket, they didn't even know what they had… and that's how I feel. Like a limited edition, tweed, expensive, rare Chanel jacket, just growing mildew on it. Cat piss on it on the curb like trash and unappreciated and now I'm thinking, can the jacket be salvaged? Can the jacket be restored? Would it be appreciated and valued elsewhere? Like a consignment shop? Can it be restored?"

Everyone is silent. I am glaring at the floor in disbelief.

"We got your back with whatever you want to do going forward, Jay, whatever your next step will be," Jena says.

The ladies agree. "That's right," Tina adds.

I look up and smile a little smile. "Well, my next step right now will be another sip of the good stuff!" I jump up and Kayla gives me a quick supportive hug. I make my way to the spread to make a snack plate. Pillar keeps my drink cup steady as she pours my drink.

We continue on. Mary J. Blige is on the playlist and the mood is beginning to go back up. The vibe is chill—and then we all hear a knock at the door.

"Is anybody expecting anyone?" Jena asks.

"Nope."

"Not me."

"See who it is!"

"Who could that be?"

"I ain't taking no walk-ins!" we all reply in unison.

I look out the door and I see a familiar face. It's Anthony Grant! Nisa's business partner. I also see an Asian guy and a young lady who appears to be ethnically ambiguous. Anthony goes by Tony and he puts up a hand to wave. "Hey!"

"Oh wow, its Tony! Nisa's business partner!" I say excitedly. I buzz them in and Tony opens the door. The young lady steps inside first and then the young man.

Tony is last to step foot inside Jay's Beauty Salon. Tall and strikingly handsome. His locs are pulled back, he is wearing a navy blue suit, and I start toward him with my arms reaching for a hug. I hear the ladies gasp. These ladies love a fine black man. To this day, Kayla says that she heard the beginning of the song, "You Send Me Swinging," by Mint Condition when she first laid eyes on him.

As I turn around to introduce Tony to the group, I notice Tina is fixing her bangs, Pillar is sipping her drink looking over the top of her glasses like a naughty librarian. Kayla is standing there with her mouth open as she clutches her pearl necklace as if lust itself was going to rip it from her neck. Nakia is wiping crumbs from her cheeks and mouth as she stands there in shock. Pamela turns her dryer off, lifts it up and gives a grin. Jena is standing with a gaze, she begins to smile as she puts her left hand to her chest as if to calm herself. Yes, this man is *that* fine!

"Ladies, I would like to introduce you all to Anthony Grant. Nisa's business partner."

"Good lord," Kayla mumbles to Nakia. "Who is this man? And why has Nisa kept him hidden?"

"Hey ladies, you all can just call me Tony. It's a pleasure to meet all of you and Nisa tells me that the Friday crew is legendary and exclusive so, we feel privileged to even get in the door!" Tony says jokingly. The ladies are hysterical with laughter. You would have thought he was Dave Chappelle, the way they were cracking up. It's obvious, they're feeling him. He continues, "This is Camille, my assistant."

"Hello everyone."

"And this is Yuto of Dynasty Travel Agency."

"Hi everybody, nice to meet you all!" Yuto says. "We are here to surprise you all with a gift from Nisa, so if you all could find a seat together, Camille is going to set up the video on the laptop."

The ladies begin to take a seat as they become excited about the surprise. "I wonder what's going on."

"What is up?"

"I hope we get to see Nisa."

I have a question for Tony while everyone is getting settled. "Tony, what is going on in here? Nisa…" I whisper, "is coming tomorrow, is she not?"

"Yeah!" he begins to whisper as he leads me away from the group. "She'll be arriving tomorrow as planned, super early, I think 5:00 a.m. She planned all of this for your birthday."

Camille announces that the recording is all set to play. Tony and I walk over to the waiting area to stand and watch. It begins. It's Nisa on the screen.

"Peace and light, Friday Crew! I hope that all of you are doing well. I am so excited to make this announcement. Now, just to be clear, you all will need to sign a waiver for privacy. No social media, etcetera. Okay? Do not share anything heard here today. So, for Jadirah's birthday… I have decided that we should all take an all-expense paid trip to… Dubai!"

The group begins to cheer as Nisa's recording continues. Jena tries to quiet everyone down, "Quiet! Shhh everybody, she's giving details."

"The plan is to vacation for seven days, so prepare accordingly with your family and work so that you don't miss out. If you do not have your passport please make arrangements to get that done as soon as possible. We are going to have a ball and turn up with our girl. She could use a break!" Nisa adds jokingly. "Now, Yuto and Camille will fill you in on all the details. I love you all very much and I miss you. Take care!" The video fades out.

"Oh my God, we're going to Dubai!"

The crew begins to celebrate with delight. Pillar busts a happy dance while Jena and Kayla share a hug. Tina is wiping tears from her eyes. These ladies work so hard, they deserve this trip. I deserve this trip. Pamela comes up to me and gives me a hug.

"This is awesome!" she says. Yuto and Camille begin talking with Jena first about the details.

"Congratulations, ladies," Tony says with a smile to the group.

"No, thank *you*, baby!" Nakia replies.

"Yes!" Pillar adds.

"Jadirah, can we go somewhere and talk in private?" Tony asks.

"Yeah, yeah. To the break room, okay?"

As Tony and I slide over to the break room, I begin to wonder what this conversation could be about. I notice also that Tony has not set his bag down. We get to the break room and I immediately shut the door and lock it. I know how private Nisa is and clearly she has sent a message with her business partner.

I take a seat. Tony takes a seat on one of the bar stools. He set the bag on the countertop. He then begins to unzip the leather bag and asks me how I've been feeling. I tell him that I'm anxious. Anxious to see what this is about.

"Nisa wanted me to talk to you today." He pulls out a navy blue folder and hands it to me. "We are prepared to make you an offer." I begin to look over the paperwork in the folder and it appears to be a contract. An agreement and a check. I exhale, shake my head and close my eyes.

Tony begins in an authoritative voice, "Now look, Jay, just want to be clear so there is no confusion. You don't have to make a decision right now, I am aware of that. You may need time to think about this proposition."

I begin to laugh a hearty laugh. Tony looks confused. "So, Nisa wants to buy my shop… Jay's Beauty Salon…" I pause and stand up.

"Do you need to speak to your husband? Is that figure ok?"

I am silent. I am thinking.

"I know that you have been a stylist most of your life —"

I interrupt. "No, Tony, I'm cool. So Nisa wants to buy the shop. Looks like she's trying to retire me from the looks of this check right here!" I chuckle as I look over the paperwork.

"She's a businesswoman, but she is also a concerned, devoted friend. You don't have to work if you don't want to, ok? Or you can take time on a sabbatical, work once a week? Whatever you want to do. No rush whatsoever."

I shake my head. I look over at Tony. "You know, I've been doing hair since I was sixteen."

He nods.

"Do you have a pen?" I ask.

Clearly my decisiveness has shocked Tony. He nods slowly and goes into his bag for a pen. "You don't want to speak to your attorney or your staff?" he hands me the pen, almost reluctantly.

"No, Tony, I don't. Everything will be fine. Nisa is a damn psychic out this piece, she knew I would take the deal! She has known for a while that I am tired," I say as I'm signing the contracts, selling my salon to my best friend.

"What do you tell your husband?"

I hand Tony the signed documents and his pen.

"I don't know, I'll come up with something," I say in a nonchalant manner. "He's going to need some help. Are you coming over for dinner tomorrow with Nisa?"

Tony sighs reluctantly and narrows his eyes.

"Please, Tony, he has this app that he's been working on and he just needs someone to listen to his ideas."

Tony's body language is all apprehensive. "I typically charge by the hour for consultation service of any kind, Jadirah."

"I know."

"I'll do it for you, I'll listen to his ideas."

"Okay, thank you! Thank you so much, just humor him it doesn't have to get too deep."

"No problem, let's get back out onto the floor." He stands and gets the door for me.

Everyone is just about finished with all of their paperwork, I check my phone and I have three missed calls from Carlos. I decide to call in case it's about the children. I make the call and he answers on the first ring: "Hey."

"What's up? Is everything okay?"

"Yeah, the kids are okay, I was just trying to see what time you would be done?"

"I'll be finished up in about an hour and a half. It's the Friday Crew so…"

"Oh, ok… so it's ladies night. I got you. Alright then, I'll see you later."

"Alright, bye." I call Pamela over so that I can begin finishing her style service.

"Jay, I'm going to start cleaning up, it's 10 o'clock, sis!" Jena says.

"Okay, thank you!" I reply.

Meanwhile, Nakia has a few questions for Tony as they enjoy the last bit of refreshments. "I noticed your accent! Where are you from?" Nakia sips her drink, awaiting Tony's response.

"I'm from New York, uptown," he replies.

"Brooklyn right here!" Pillar announces.

A tipsy Nakia raps, "Is Brooklyn in da house?"

"Without a doubt!" Pillar calls out. "I grew up in public housing. Are you from the projects, Tony?" Pillar asks.

"No, actually, I grew up in a Brownstone with my mother and father. I have three brothers."

"A Brownstone? Y'all must have been rich or hit the lotto," Nakia begins to pry.

"No, my dad was a Jamaican immigrant so he had maybe four jobs? My mother is a teacher, she knows all about hard work and how important education is. She was born and raised in Jim Crow-era Georgia.”

"So it's not a myth about Jamaicans? Do they all work like crazy?” Kayla asks.

"I wouldn't know, I don't know *all* of the Jamaicans. I've seen a couple lazy ones that will only…” Tony looks around to make sure everyone is paying attention, “work *one* job!” he finishes jokingly. His sense of humor is amazing. He continues to talk to the ladies and make small talk as I finish curling Pamela's hair.

I notice Yuto and Camille are packing their bags up and Jena and Kayla are just about finished cleaning up. Tina is ready to leave. She stops by my station to ask if I need any help with anything. I tell her that it's all good, all is covered and I thank her for making today special. As I finish styling Pamela's hair, she realizes where she's seen Tony before.

"The B.B.S! That's where I recognize you from, Tony!”

"What's that?” Kayla asks.

"The Black Business Seminar, it's a group that I'm a part of that informs about financial literacy, managing debt, networking and entrepreneurial excellence,” Tony answers.

"That's right! I've seen a few of the summit discussions on YouTube,” Pamela says as I remove her styling cape.

The ladies are paying close attention now. They find Tony interesting and it shows. I begin sweeping off my workstation as the chatting continues. It's getting very late and my buzz is wearing off. I click off my side lamp to show the ladies that I'm ready to start my shop duties: finish up for the day, do my dance, lock up and go home.

Tony notices. "Yeah, so be sure to subscribe to stay posted on other events and follow me on the 'Gram!” He begins to walk away from the group and toward me. "Hey, we better get going, it's getting late,” Tony says as we quickly embrace. "Hit me up if you need anything, ok?”

"Okay, thank you so much!" I look over to say goodbye to Camille and Yuto. "It was nice to meet you both, thank you for everything, what a wonderful surprise."

"It's nice to meet you also, we're just glad to help," Camille adds with a smile.

"Good to meet you too, you all have a great night," Yuto says.

The ladies all bid farewell to Tony, Camille, and Yuto. As they grab their coats, they chat it up as they prepare to leave. I think to myself how incredibly exciting today has been. I don't even care that Ja'Nay is leaving the shop. I hear my friends' laughter as I put my shears and bobby pins away. There is a scent of hairspray, women's fragrances, wine, and flowers in the air. The evening is complete with a clear sky and a full moon.

As I look over at these ladies, I feel a sense of gratitude. I will not reveal to them that I've sold the salon. Maybe I'll still come in to service this group on Fridays to keep loose. I love them. They make me forget what happened to me before and trust in what is happening here and now. Nisa was a hero tonight on many different levels. I want to call, but I know that airplane mode has been placed on her phone.

The ladies grab their bags, keys, and come over to give me a hug. "Love ya sis."

"Bye, babe."

"Love you."

"Have a blessed one."

"What a night."

"Love you."

"Call me if you need anything."

"Goodnight ladies. I love you all so much."

Jena stays to finish helping me with my shop duties. "Hey, sis, I got it covered, it's late," I say.

"Are you sure? I can stay and we could walk out together?" Jena replies.

"Jena…" I place a tentative hand upon her arm. "I want you to go home and get some rest or we gonna fight!"

"Alright, alright! I don't want to argue." We laugh it out.

"Ok, love you, Jena. Thanks for putting all of this together."

"You know I got you," Jena says with a smile. We embrace and my sister cousin tells me that she is proud of me.

Jena starts walking toward the front door and opens it to leave. I watch her as she goes to her car. She gets in the driver seat and waves. She is in safely. I wave back. I lock the door and pull the wall panel in front of the glass front door. I close the blinds and pull the curtains closed. I am glad to have had fun with my girls tonight, but for what I have to do next, I need complete solitude.

Now I'm certainly not Laurie Ann Gibson, Paula Abdul or Ciara, but… I dance. Hard. In a spiritual, celebratory way when no one is around. I used to do Hip Hop dance and Jazz dance when I was younger. But when I dance, it's soul, it's spiritual, it's in pure gratitude, and it is my heart's joy. It's an outlet for my Avatar.

What will I select for tonight? As I check through my playlist, I think to myself that I want to pick up the pace. We've been listening to Jill, Erykah, and Mary all night and they always speak healing to my soul. But… tonight?

HIP HOP. I was born a Hip-Hop-head and I need a strong beat to dance to so I may release. "So let's see… Quiet Storm, Electric Relaxation, Slam, hmmm… These are all good ones, Jadirah. Ahh! Here we go." I queue it up and close my eyes and wait for the beat to drop.

"Alls my life I had to fight nigga, Alls my life I— Hard times like, Yah! Bad trips like, Yah! Nazareth, I'm fucked up. Homie, you fucked up. But if God got us, then we gon' be alright." I start to dance and rap along with Kendrick. I grab the broom while dancing and I begin to sweep the waiting area. As I dance I start to think about my childhood as I feel my soul open up. These

lyrics have always triggered my memories. My thoughts of survival and vitality. My mind begins to surf through my past. I think of walking as a little girl with my two sisters and my little brother. As we were walking down the street to our Arabic lessons and some grown woman spat upon my youngest sister and called us "heathens."

As I dance, other memories start to flow. I remember going to choir practice with Grandma Robinson. "Sit up straight, girl, and leave your tights alone. Don't be fidgety." I still hear her voice as I reminisce.

Thoughts of hopscotch with Nisa and my sisters fly by. Riding my bike, getting bullied and getting into fist fights because you aren't allowed to be "different" than everyone else in the hood. Not allowed to be prideful or smart. Not allowed to speak a different language other than English. Not allowed to talk about your family's achievements. I learned to subdue myself, to diminish my gifts, to fit into what everyone else thought I should be.

I cannot believe I find myself going back into that space in my marriage.

I open my eyes. The song is still going. I dance to the broom closet to grab the mirror cleaner and a rag. As I wipe the salon mirrors and continue to rhyme along with Kendrick, I am thrilled at the thought of seeing my sister friend tomorrow. It's unbelievable that she just bought my salon today. Do I want to speak to Carlos about it?

No.

But, I know that I'll have to eventually. Maybe Nisa feels responsible for so much that has taken place in our life together because she was the one who introduced us back in the day. I remember Jakka telling me that Carlos wasn't ready to be married. I was pregnant and scared. I thought that getting married would fix everything. As I slow down from being tired of wiping the mirror, I catch my eyes in the reflection.

I look tired. Beat. Dark circles under my eyes and scars all over the right side of my face from the fall last week. I stare at myself for just a few seconds before cracking a smile.

"Survivor!" I say aloud. "Jadirah, you are your ancestors' wildest dreams." I close my eyes and listen to the song's end. I turn the music off, grab my things, put on my jacket and pause before I hit the light switch.

Every night, I say the same gratitude prayer: "Father, I thank you for this space. I thank you for all of the blessings. Amen." Lights out.

I have a shocking revelation; I never realized just how much I resent my marriage until it's time to go home. Things are so different now.

FOUR

Wild Flower

My natural rhythms awake me at exactly 4:37 a.m. I know this feeling. It's like the first day of school. Today is Saturday, right? Okay, let's get it, I need to get up and pee.

I'm going into work today but only for a few hours. I have Dr. Heinz at 9:00 a.m. and Imani at 7:00 a.m., then I have to go grocery shopping for Grandma Faye and for dinner tonight. As I turn the water on to shower, I begin to wrap my hair up, I hear Carlos fumbling around in the bedroom. I lock the door. I know his schedule. I know what he wants, but he ain't gon' get it!

He knocks.

"Yeah!" I call out.

"Morning, beautiful."

I roll my eyes, "Morning, I'll be right out."

"Well I was… wanted to come in there with you."

I don't respond.

"I didn't see you at all yesterday, babe. I just want to be around you."

I feel bad for him, I do love him. I just don't have a song in my heart for him anymore. "Hey, Los, I'll be right out, I gotta get ready for work. Okay?" I listen for a response and then I hear his footsteps going away.

I shower, brush my teeth and get dressed. Smells of coffee brewing in the kitchen. I'm clear about what Carlos want to do. I'm going to avoid him and pretend that I have to go into work early today. But first, I must make my morning prayers and kiss all of my children goodbye.

As I approach the kitchen to bid farewell to Carlos, I notice that he isn't in there. He must be in the restroom on the lower level. I open the door to the lower level. "Hey, Los, I'm gone," I announce without disturbing the entire house.

"Alright, baby. I love you."

I pause. "Alright, you too! Peace."

As I head out of the front door, I notice that it's a cool, brisk morning. I am bundled up. I feel good about today. I check my phone for the time and it is now 5:28 a.m. I don't have to get to work until 7:00 a.m. so I'll head over to the Coffee House for a while to ease into my day. I arrive at the Coffee House and I order a latte and a morning bun.

"For here or to go?" the barista asks.

"Mmm… you know what? Here is fine."

"Okay."

I pay for my order and look around for the best seat in the space. I choose the spot right next to the fireplace. There are only two other customers here, so I know that my order won't take very long. My name is called and I collect my drink and my breakfast, I take a seat and I exhale. I hate that I don't feel comfortable at home anymore. I enjoy my solitude. Right now, in here, I can think. And right now, I think I will call my dad. I know he's up. I dial and he picks up on the second ring.

"Yes?" he answers

"Blessed rising, Daddy."

"Oh, Jadirah! Blessed rising and peace be with you! How are you feeling, baby?"

"I'm blessed, Daddy, I feel grateful. I'll be heading into work soon, off early today though."

"Yeah, I know, your mama told me that it's your turn to ride out into the boondocks to take Mama her grocery list!" he laughs.

"Yes! I've been summoned by the Supreme Mother herself!"

"It'll be good for you. It will be good for your spirit."

I become silent for a moment. "What do you and Mom have going on for today?"

"Well, your mom has a garden club meeting and the line dance and whatever else she's doing. But you know, I have a gig tonight at Smitty's!"

"That's right, Mom did mention that!"

"You all should come through, Jay!"

"You know what? I might swing through and I might bring a mystery guest with me."

"Alright good! That's what I like to hear."

I can hear a smile in his voice.

"Alright Daddy, I'm going to let you get back to it. Love you!"

"Love you too, baby girl. Peace."

"Peace."

I end the call, gather my things and head to the salon. I hop into my old, faithful Beemer and I begin to think of how I avoided Carlos this morning. I know that he would like to talk and there is a great deal that I would've liked to say. There is so much to unpack emotionally as well as logically. I know he'll become defensive and allow his personal feelings to interfere. I simply do not have the energy for nonsense today.

I turn my stereo to the throwback station and "Wildflower" by New Birth is playing. I turn the music up and close my eyes for a second. I absolutely love this song. As I sing along and I drive, I begin to reminisce about growing up in Philly. I think about the old neighborhood, going to elementary school, the old restaurants and, of course, how Nisa and I used to get into so much trouble as children.

My father and her father were good friends. They met when my dad played in a band while in New York. Nisa's father was the door security at the club where my father played on a regular basis. His name was Jeffrey but we all called him Uncle Jeff. He was about six foot three, handsome brown-skinned man with big muscles and a gap in his smile. He was the only man in the hood who knew how to do real karate like Jim Kelly.

Nisa's mother was the most beautiful woman I had ever seen. She was from the Dominican Republic. Her skin was brown and her hair was long, black and curly. She spoke broken English and French. She would speak Spanish loud and quickly when she was angry. Her name was Ana. Every time we would tag along with my dad to visit, Ms. Ana would be cooking.

My mother would never come to visit because she would always say that Ms. Ana was "loose" and she had "no class." It was rumored that Uncle Jeff had cleaned her up from prostitution back in Spanish Harlem in the '70s when she was about eighteen years old. I didn't care about any of that. She was always nice to me and my siblings. She would say to us in her thick accent, "American Negro and Dominican...?" She would then hold up both hands, clapping them together and clasp her fingers together and say, "Are one. Stronger together... Okay?" she would smile.

She would cook so much but maintained such a great figure. Nisa's brother, Junior, was always outside playing basketball or football. He was the greatest dancer of all and he was the funniest kid on earth. I hear that he'll be out of prison in about two months.

My father named Nisa when she was born. I've known her my entire life. She's ten months older than me. As a child, she was the most athletic, smartest, and most charismatic leader in school. She was so funny. But she had a temper. A temper that my sisters and I would hate to see and sometimes she would curse. We were good girls, we wouldn't be caught dead cursing. Nisa was bold enough to cuss bullies out in school. She would be slick enough to make sure adults weren't around, though.

When we were in fifth grade, the most devastating event took place. Uncle Jeff was leaving the bar one night, headed for home. He was always getting harassed by the police because he was so muscular and they knew that he was a black belt in martial arts. They would give him the business on any given day. He got into an altercation with crooked cops on his way home and was shot four times for "resisting arrest." The neighborhood went mad over his death. When the pictures were released of the two cops, they were beaten pretty badly. He was a peaceful man, but the cops always challenged him, for no reason other than that he was a big black dude.

It destroyed Ms. Ana and she started drinking heavily and using cocaine. She even got fired from her waitress job. Nisa and Junior spent a lot of time with our family for dinners or a hot bath if the water was turned off at Ms. Ana's. When Ms. Ana got a new boyfriend, Junior moved out and Nisa was furious with him. Ms. Ana's new boyfriend was a creep and a drug dealer. Nisa would go to choir practice sometimes with me and Grandma Robinson. She would go to Jumu'ah on some Fridays with us and Daddy. She had become our adopted sister while Ms. Ana was strung out.

When we reached sixth grade, her confidence had started to return after the loss. She told me that her mother had bought her a new bed and she felt that things would begin to get back to normal. After about two months into the new school year, she told me about a strange occurrence that had been happening Saturday nights.

"Well, do you wanna talk about it?" I ask.

"Yeah, let's go out on your porch." When we arrive on the front porch, we sit on the lawn chairs. "I've been waking up in the back seat of his car."

"Who, Robert? Ana's new boyfriend?"

"Yeah!"

"I don't get it, why?"

"Well," Nisa scoots in close and looks around as she lowers her voice, "You can't tell nobody!"

"Okay, okay! What happened?"

"Robert lets me have whiskey sometimes."

"Eeew, how did it taste?"

"It's nasty and it burns your throat!"

"Ugh."

"No, but check this out, Jadirah, I have just one drink, right. I pass out on the couch or in the big chair and then, I wake up in the back seat of his car?!?"

"What?"

"Crazy, right?"

"Well, Nisa, are you sleep walking?"

"I don't think so. I know what drunk feels like, though. You feel dizzy and it makes your coochie hurt!"

"What!"

"Yep. Every time I come back in the house he's sitting there with his boys in the living room watching TV and he always says the same thing… *Where you been? We was gonna start lookin for you, bad girl!* and I'm just dizzy and want to lay down in my bed!"

"Did you tell your mom?"

"What? That I was drinking whiskey? Hell no! If I—"

Just as Nisa was speaking about her recent experiences, Shaniqua Marshall and Tamika Laurence walk up to my yard and interrupt. "I'm gonna fight you at school on Tuesday, Jadirah!" Shaniqua blurts out.

Nisa stands up from her chair behind my mother's plants. "Shut up, you fat red pimple-faced ugly stank-breath bitch! You ain't gon' do shit, bitch!" she yells.

"Shut up, Nisa! You think you so tough, ain't nobody even talkin' to you!" Tamika responds.

"Yeah, ain't nobody tryin to fight your crazy ass, Nisa! Jadirah think she better than everybody else!"

Just then my mother storms out onto the porch in a panic. "What is going on out here!? What do you girls think you're doing, Nisa, using language like that?"

Nisa says nothing but points to Shaniqua and Tamika and they're moving away from the fence and beginning to move along down the street.

"You girls don't come back around here making trouble!" my mother announces. By this time, they're running down the street.

"Nisa…" my mother begins.

"It wasn't my fault, they tryna fight Jadirah at school so, I cussed 'em out and told dem no they wasn't!"

My mom sighs. She shakes her head. "Y'all get in the house."

We go inside.

"Sit down on the couch."

We sit and we prepare to get an earful.

"Look, ladies, I am not raising y'all to be savages. You all need to use your etiquette lessons when dealing with these children that have no home training. You all need to be civilized." She then looks at Nisa and grabs her hands and looks her in the eyes. "Look, baby, I know that things have been rough. I know that you are angry."

Nisa looks down.

Mom gently tips her chin back up to eye level. "We love you, Nisa, and we will always be here for you. But honey, I don't play that in my house! Okay?"

"Yes ma'am," Nisa replies.

"Alright now, y'all go on and get cleaned up and set the table, honey."

My mother has always been a very proper woman. She went to charm school as a little girl and she has always been a classy lady. She never wanted us to behave like our peers. She was from a well-to-do family and she consistently displayed it. Her side of the family never approved of my father.

A few weeks pass. School was a typical drag. Out of nowhere, Nisa shows up to school one day with a bruise on her face. My sisters Fatimah and Amirrah saw her first when we were approaching the school.

"What happened to you?" Fatimah asks.

"Nuthin, got into a fight. You should see the other bitch, I fucked her face up!" Nisa replies.

"Oh no... Nisa, why are you always getting into trouble?" Amirrah asks in concern and frustration. "Was it someone we know? Is she in high school with me?"

"No, Amirrah, just drop it, alright!"

"Whatever," my oldest sister Amirrah says, annoyed.

We continue walking to our school. Amirrah's high school is down the block. She drops us off and keeps going.

"Y'all be good, don't get suspended again, Nisa!!" Amirrah calls out as she walks away.

Nisa rolls her eyes and sucks her teeth in frustration at Amirrah's authoritative tone. We continue to walk when Nisa notices some of Fatimah's friends and makes a suggestion. "Fatimah, there go Tasha and LaToya! Go see what they doin!"

Fatima runs ahead to catch up, Tasha and LaToya greet Fatimah as they talk mess to the boys.

Really, Nisa needed to speak to me in private. "Jadirah, what I need to say, you can't tell nobody, okay?"

"Okay Nisa, wussup?"

"I didn't get jumped. I just said that so Amirrah would get off my back."

We walk silently for a few steps and then Nisa stops and grabs my arm to stop. She then looks around to see if anyone is around to overhear our conversation.

"Jadirah I… I think I might've gotten raped," she says quietly and very seriously. I gasp and I look into her eyes and can tell that she is not kidding. She is dead-ass serious.

"Really? By who?" I say with concern laced in every word. I'm shaking.

"It was my mom's boyfriend, Robert. I had a drink with him and passed out again except, I was in the back seat of his Chevy and I was waking up and he was on top of me hunchin!"

"Oh my goodness, Nisa!" I begin to well up with tears.

"I looked at him as I was waking up and I said, *What are you doing,* and he looked at me, and he looked scared! And he punched me! And I passed back out!" I can see the fear in her eyes as she describes her very first sexual encounter. Ever.

I cover my mouth. I can't think of any words that might comfort her. Oddly, Nisa is not crying. Her eyes are wide open and she is staring into the distance. "Are you gonna tell your mom?" I ask.

Nisa doesn't respond. She's out of it.

"NISA!?! Snap out of it!" I grab her arm.

She closes her eyes and shakes her head.

"Nisa, I think we should call the cops!"

"No! I hate the fuckin cops!"

"Stop cussin, Nisa! We gotta figure something out. What are you gonna do?"

"I think I might have an idea. We better go into the school, but look, if anybody asks… just tell them I got into a fight okay?"

"Okay, anything you say," I reply reluctantly.

We go on into the school and go to our lockers. I guess at this point you can tell that something is wrong, just by looking at my face. Nisa notices as she puts her coat away. "Don't, Jadirah!"

"Don't what, Nisa? We should probably get help!" I say.

"No. Don't look like that! You have to learn how to pretend, hide your face and act normal!"

We begin to walk to our separate homerooms. All the while Nisa is smiling and making slick remarks to other students as if nothing ever happened. She actually gave me advice on how to conceal my true concern for her and her situation. I have never been a good pretender. Nisa keeps secrets very well.

Robert should be in jail for hurting my friend, I think to myself. He should be exposed for what he has done and should be ashamed.

"Alright, Jay, I'll see you at lunch?"

"Yeah," I reply very dryly.

"Okay, remember!" Nisa then puts her index finger up to her lips and says, "Shhh." I just nod and walk into my classroom.

Class goes by and is a complete drag because I can't seem to focus. I keep thinking about lunch period. What is Nisa's plan? I wonder what's going to happen.

Lunch period finally arrives and I am anxious. I walk into the cafeteria and look around for Nisa. I feel a tap on my shoulder and I turn around. It's Shaniqua, Tamika, and two other little peons trying to look tough.

"It's Tuesday, Jadirah, I'm gon' fight you after school!" Shaniqua says.

"You ain't gon' do nuthin!" I reply.

A small crowd starts to develop. "Imma give you a bloody nose after school."

"You ain't gonna do shit, Shaniqua," Nisa says from behind me.

"Nisa, why you always runnin' your mouth, ain't nobody even checkin' for you, stupid!" Shaniqua says.

"Shaniqua, you the one that is stupid. First of all, you always messin' with Jadirah and she don't bother nobody. And you just mad cause you smell like pee and you mad cuz you ugly… Bitch!"

"Ohhh," the crowd replies.

Just then, Mrs. Williams, the assistant principal, walks over and breaks it all up. "What's going on over here, people? Break it up and be seated! I have no problems writing up detention slips."

As the crowd disperses, Nisa grabs my arm and takes me to the lunch table way over by the trash can. No one ever sits over here because it stinks! Smart move for privacy, though. As we sit, I lay my lunch bag down and begin to unfasten the snap.

"No! We ain't eating over here! I gotta tell you the plan." Nisa leans in close. As her eyes widen, she takes one last glance around us to make sure that no one is around to hear us. And then she says: "We're going to kill Robert!"

I gasp. Clearly she's joking. I don't believe her for one second. I suck my teeth and blurt out, "You play too much, why would you even say that?"

"I'm serious, Jadirah. Look at my face! He's been raping me, he gotta go!"

"Lower your voice, Nisa!"

"Jadirah, if you are in, be to my mom's house at ten o'clock Saturday night. I'm gonna make it look like an accident."

"I don't wanna do nothing. If I come over there, I ain't doing anything! Okay?"

"If you're my friend, you'll have my back," Nisa says as her eyes look up from mine. She starts a whole different conversation on the spot. "Now if you would just let me borrow your notes from science class, I would feel better about my grade because…"

Mrs. Williams interrupts the phony conversation. "What are you ladies doing all the way over here?" Mrs. Williams says, approaching us. She stands right next to Nisa.

Nisa looks up reluctantly. "We're just talkin' about science class. I took bad notes and I need to borrow Jadirah's."

Mrs. Williams folds her arms and raises an eyebrow. "Is that right? I hardly believe that, everyone knows that you take unbelievable notes… Miss Honor Roll!" Nisa looks down. "What happened to your face, little one?"

"I got jumped."

"By who?"

"No one from this school. Some kids from my neighborhood."

Mrs. Williams rolls her eyes. She takes a seat next to me. "Nisa, you are such a bright young lady. Talented and charismatic. Please learn to control your temper. I want to see you rise up outta this ghetto mess out here, baby. Okay?"

"Okay."

"Alright now, y'all come over back away from the dumpster area. It stinks over here, sheesh!"

We get up and head over toward the more populated section of the school cafeteria. As we sit to begin to eat our lunch, we are silent. I think to myself, *I'm going to help Nisa, I'm not going to do anything bad but I'm going to help her get justice.*

The rest of the school week is a complete drag. Saturday finally arrives. I've been thinking about this day all week. I tell my mother that I'm going to Nisa's to braid her hair tonight after dinner, which is usually the case. I have my mother's permission to go to Nisa's.

Nisa needs my support. We are like sisters. She is a victim of physical and sexual abuse. I feel that I have an obligation to help her because she can trust me. I intend to aid in her healing or to end all of the pain that she has had to endure in her short thirteen years. She is not on this planet to pleasure some sick perverted man. Uncle Jeff is no longer here to protect and guide her. Ms. Ana is always drunk or high. *I will have my friend's back!*

Do I have the courage to stand tall for her? Thoughts rush through my head as I search for ideas. Maybe we can knock him over the head and drag him down to the police station. As I reach Nisa's house, I notice her sitting on the front stoop. "Hey!" I call out as I light-jog up to the stairs. Nisa stands up and stops me from going into the townhome.

"Hey, he's not here yet. Let's walk up to the end of the block. I want to show you something."

We begin down the block and walk silently for a few steps when Nisa pulls some white pills out of her pocket. She shows them to me.

"What are those?"

"Knockout pills!"

"What?"

"Knockout pills, mickeys! I'm gonna fix him the same kinda drink he been fixin' me! I got these from Frankie."

"So when he passes out, then what? I'm not going to do nothin crazy!"

"You don't have to do nuthin crazy, Jadirah…" Nisa pauses and takes a deep breath. "After he passes out you just put lighter fluid on his shirt. I can't do it 'cause I'll have the matches."

"Okay, are you sure that this is going to work?"

"Yes. He's gotta pay for what he has been doing to me."

I agree. Unfortunately, I'm not sold on this plan of setting a man on fire! We turn to walk back to Nisa's house and we see Robert and one of his friends pull up and go into the house. They didn't even notice that we were walking. Before we go inside, I hesitate.

"What's wrong?" Nisa asks. I don't reply. I simply look down. She grabs my arm and says, "Look at me." I look up. "Be strong no matter what, okay?" she says firmly.

I exhale and nod. Where does this little girl get all of this fearlessness from? Did she inherit Uncle Jeff's courage when his soul left this earth?

We go inside and Robert and his buddy are turning the radio on. They have sandwiches and liquor on the coffee table. The front room is a mess. I don't even want to see the kitchen.

"Hey now, girls! Ahh, you all are getting so big," Robert's friend Moe says.

"You stayin' out of trouble, Nisa? No more fights, alright," Robert says, pretending to act like her father.

"We're goin up to my room to study, c'mon, J," Nisa says as we turn to climb the stairs to her room. As we pass Ms. Ana's room, we notice a bucket on the floor next to her bed, the small TV is blaring, and Ms. Ana is on the bed, asleep. Drunk. "Don't even worry about her, she fine. She drunk and asleep," Nisa adds as we pass.

We get to Nisa's bedroom and it is impeccable. The bed is made up, her clothes are neatly folded and her dolls and games are put away neatly on top of her dresser.

"Nisa, you lucky you got your own room, it's always so neat and clean in here."

"It's the only room I can keep clean. These niggas up in here are cool with living like animals. When I grow up my entire house will always be CLEAN AS A WHISTLE!" she says excitedly. "And besides, my daddy used to say, *When you clean up the house, it takes your mind off of everything.*"

We sit silently for a few moments.

Nisa gets up and goes to her bedside table and pulls out a small bottle. She walks over to me and hands it to me.

"All you have to do is spray this all over his shirt when he falls asleep, okay?"

"Got it."

"I'm going to go downstairs and fix them both a drink. You wait up here," Nisa says calmly.

I crack the bedroom door to listen. I hear the stereo and the television blaring. Then I hear Nisa. "Hey y'all!" she says cheerfully. "Who wants a taste of the good stuff?"

"Pour me some!"

"Put some ice in mine."

These unsuspecting fools have no idea what Nisa is about to pull. Surely they would never guess that a sixth-grader would plan to drug them.

As I move away from the door, I begin to look around the bedroom. Nisa has old clothes with square patches in them. I pick up a dress with a perfect square cut out of it and I put it back down. I hear footsteps coming down the hall and I stand still. The door opens and it's Nisa.

"Whew," I breathe a sigh of relief.

"Whatchu doin? Goin through my stuff?"

"Yeah, what are you workin on?"

"I keep my clothes that I can't fit anymore and I cut some of it up and I'm going to sew it onto this jean skirt." She goes to her dresser to pull out her knee length denim skirt.

"Aww that's gonna be cute!"

"Yeah, and nobody else will have a skirt like it! It's gonna be a one of a kind, custom skirt. I oughta make a matching hat!"

"I can't wait to see it finished."

"I'm gonna be the best fashion designer. I'm so glad your mom taught us how to sew without a machine."

"I know, Mommy know how to do everything."

We grow quiet for a bit. Nisa decides to go back downstairs to see if Robert and his friend have passed out. She leaves the bedroom door open so that I can hear. I know that it's starting to get late. I become a little anxious waiting for Nisa. And then, I hear footsteps, quick footsteps up the stairs.

"Jadirah, Jadirah!" Nisa whispers. I step out into the hallway. "C'mon, let's move fast," Nisa says.

"Okay let's go."

We move quietly but quickly down the hallway stairs and I'm trying not to think of anything. I am helping my friend and I am with her all the way.

My heart is beating fast and there is an indescribable adrenaline rush that takes hold. This is it! The moment of truth.

We get down to the living room and Nisa pauses to reach into her pocket. I glance at her and I keep moving. I pull the small bottle of lighter fluid out. I open it as I'm walking. I walk right up to Robert as he's slumped over, asleep in Uncle Jeff's big chair. *A son of a bitch that rapes littles girls!* I don't even blink, I march right up to him and spray his shirt in the chest area, drop the small bottle and zip right past Nisa and stand at the front door.

"Nisa hurry up!" I whisper in a panic.

She looks over at me very calmly and says, "Alright." She then approaches Robert's sleeping body with glaring eyes. I've never seen her like this before. She takes out the book of matches and strikes one. She stands back and tosses it onto Robert's shirt.

It catches fire immediately. Robert is still knocked out! I go outside on the stoop and look in through the window in a panic! Nisa is standing in front of him expressionless, watching the fire burn through his clothes. Calmly.

I do believe I met Nisa's soul in that very moment. Fearless and restless for justice by any means. A child looking to make things right. I was in awe of her and afraid of her at the same time.

"What are you doing!?" Robert's friend Moe says. He has awakened in a total panic. Nisa looks at him, startled. I begin to run. Scared out of my mind, I hear Nisa calling from behind me. I also hear my heart beating in my ears.

I feel a sudden grip on the back of my jacket to slow me down from running. It's Nisa. I stop. "Jadirah, wait a minute!"

"We gotta get outta here! We goin' to jail!" I say, out of breath.

"No, we're not!" Nisa says, panting.

I look around and realize we are in an alley. "We can't talk here. I can't believe what just happened, Nisa!"

"Don't panic, J. Keep your mouth shut. Just go home. I'm gonna just say it was an accident. Nobody even saw you," she whispers.

"Are you sure?"

"Yeah, I'm gonna tell them it was an accident with a candle. You go home and don't say shit! You got it?"

"Yeah."

"Okay, go!"

I run home. As I look back, I notice she's walking back to her place. I know she's tough. She'll think of something. It's serious trouble! Somehow, I feel that everything will be fine.

I get home and look at the front porch. I stand silently and decide to go around back. I don't see my dad's car. *He must be at a gig tonight,* I think to myself. As I approach the back door, I realize I am sweating and my hair is disheveled. *Tidy up,* I think to myself as I straighten my clothes and hair. I open the door and I hear footsteps from upstairs. I rush to hang my coat and take my shoes off.

"Jadirah?"

"Yes, ma'am?"

"Come upstairs to my room right now! Do you know what time it is?"

I don't respond. Frightened, I run up the stairs. I get to my mother's room. She's sitting on her bed in her night clothes.

"Girl, what is the matter with you? Do you know that I was about to send your sisters down there to get you? Don't ever stay out that late! You will be on punishment for a week, you understand?" Mom yells.

"Yes ma'am. I apologize," I reply.

"I accept your apology. And what is that smell?"

I freeze and I think that I'm caught! Do I smell like lighter fluid? Do I smell like cigarettes? Yeah! I can smell cigarette smoke in my hair. Robert was smoking cigarettes. "Ms. Ana was smoking cigarettes again, Mama," I say confidently.

"Bless her heart, she's been through a lot. Other than that, she's still clean, right? I heard she's been doing good at that new job downtown."

"She looks okay."

"Alright, well, go on to bed and no more bad Jadirah mess. Goodnight."

"Yes ma'am, goodnight." I turn to go to my shared room with my little sister. I look around the dark room for my pajamas. I'm glad Fatimah is asleep. I don't want to talk at all. I quickly dress into my pajamas and climb up to the top bunkbed.

I don't sleep a wink that night. I stay up. I play out every single scenario of how the next day will be. Did Robert die? Did the house burn down? Will he stop, drop, and roll? Oh no, is Ms. Ana okay? Did Nisa get arrested? Maybe she told the firemen that she was walking with a candle and then tripped. I hope my troubled, brave friend is alright.

The next day, I get up and get dressed. My intention is to find out what happened. My mother and father are in the kitchen having coffee as they always do on Sunday morning. I am going to ask to go to check on Nisa. I walk into the kitchen fully dressed. My mother notices.

"Well, good morning, baby. Where do you think you're going all dressed?"

"Mornin' baby," Dad says.

"Good morning. I wanted to ask if I could go over Nisa's."

"Girl, did you forget? You are on punishment. No hangin' out!"

"What if I take Fatimah and Ammirah with me?" I say with concern.

"No!" Mother says sharply.

"Wait a minute, Diane," Dad says as he looks into my face. "Let me see your eyes, Jadirah."

I continue to look down at the floor. My dad prays five times a day. His vibration is always in sync with mine. He doesn't always use words to figure things out. He's tapped in and he *knows* when something is wrong. I think of something to say. *Try not to cry,* I think to myself.

"Jadirah!" Mom says.

My father gets up from the kitchen table to approach me. He tips my chin gently upward toward him. "Are you going to tell me what's going on, young lady? Let me see your eyes."

I close my eyes and break down crying.

"Baby, what's wrong!? What happened? Sit down. Now you tell us what's going on right now!" says my dad, losing his temper.

I'm so angry that I broke down. I can't snitch. What can I say to get over to check on my friend? Ok. I take a deep breath.

"Go ahead, honey," Mom says, concerned.

"I gotta protect Nisa," I say reluctantly.

"Why, what happened?"

"Ms. Ana's boyfriend tried to touch her," I say apprehensively. "He won't do nothin' if company is over there and that's why I was over there so late yesterday."

"What!" my father says furiously. "Diane, we'll be back later, c'mon Jadirah, get your coat."

I stand up to get my coat and I see my dad grab his knife and place it in his back pocket.

"Raheem, don't get yourself in trouble over no street trash!" my mother says to my father in a lowered voice.

"I just wanna talk to him, baby, we gon' be right back."

Mother nods. "Ok."

"Come on, Jadirah, let's go," Dad says with a sense of urgency.

"Yes sir."

We hop in my Dad's car and zip through the neighborhood to Ms. Ana's. "How long has this been goin on?"

"I just found out, Daddy."

"I gave my word to Jeff that I would look out for those kids if anything ever happened. Your word is your bond."

I understand everything my dad is saying. I wish I could tell him everything. But, *my* word IS my bond. We approach Ms. Ana's house and notice that she's sitting on the stoop barefoot and rocking back and forth. She's smoking a cigarette and tears are streaming down her face. She looks up and sees us pulling up. She stands and starts to walk to the car. I'm scared to death of what she's going to say.

Dad shuts the car off and immediately hops out. "Ana! What is going on? Where is your man? I need to talk to him right now!"

"Raheem, he's at the hospital! Where is Nisa, have you seen her? I'm going to lose my mind!"

"Wait, slow down, Ana. Calm down and tell me what happened!"

"Okay, okay…" Ana closes her eyes and takes a deep breath. "I had fallen asleep and Moe woke me up and said he put the fire out and that Robert was on fire! He ran out after because he said that if I called a police he would get arrested 'cause of a warrant or something… He said Nisa is a bad girl. The ambulance came and got Robert, he at the hospital." She begins to cry again.

"Alright, alright. Let's get you up to the house and get you a jacket and some shoes on."

We begin to walk back up to the townhome. Ana continues, "I don't know where my baby girl is! Raheem, will you please give me a ride to the hospital? Robert is burned very bad I want to see if he is still alive."

We make it into the house and it smells awful. The chair is partially burned and part of the carpet. Moe must've put the fire out himself. The carpet is soaking wet and it stinks.

"Okay, so grab your things and let's go," Dad calls out. "We're going to wait outside."

We go back outside and some of the neighbors have become spectators of this fire situation. "What's goin on, Willie! Have you seen little Nisa?" Dad asks one of the neighbors that he's known for some time.

"Naw man, I ain't seen nuthin. They sayin that the nigga caught fire. Fell asleep with a cigar in his mouth."

"Okay, that's what the streets is sayin?" My mind drifts off after Willie's statement. I'm thinking what if Nisa put that out as the word on the street to cover her ass! Moe was not supposed to wake up. He saw her. If Moe told Robert what happened, Nisa is in real trouble!

When we arrive at the hospital, we go to the Burn Victims Unit. The nurse tells us that Robert has survived and that they are running some tests. We can sit in the waiting area until he's ready to receive visitors.

"Jadirah, look baby, you and Ana go and sit down. I'm gonna call your mom and let her know where we are, okay?" my dad says.

"Yes sir."

We take a seat. After sitting silently for a few minutes, I notice that Ms. Ana is trembling and bouncing her leg nervously. She is a recovering addict and an alcoholic.

"Ms. Ana, you want a coffee?" I ask her.

"Yes, I do, sweetheart. Gracias," she says, glaring at the TV in the waiting area. "Black, no sugar!"

"De nada," I reply as I get up to search for the complimentary coffee. I can smell it, so it's not far. But I want to snoop around to see what I can find out. What I really want to know is, has Robert talked to the police and what does he remember? I locate the coffee station and begin to prepare Ana's cup. Two cops stand behind me and I become nervous. They chat together as I wrap up. I'm moving so quickly that I spill a little. "Ouch!"

"Be careful, little lady, this coffee is as hot as the devil," the nice police officer says with a smile.

"Okay, sorry." I start back to my seat next to Ms. Ana. I notice my father is on his way back from the payphone. "Hey Daddy!" I call out to get his attention.

"Hey, baby. Is that for me?"

"Ms. Ana. Her nerves are real bad, Daddy."

"Okay, yeah, they would be. I told everybody to look for Nisa."

"Thanks, Dad." I walk over to the waiting area. I carefully hand the coffee to Ms. Ana and I take my seat. About an hour passes when the lead nurse comes to us and says that we can see Robert. My father decides that only Ms. Ana should go in. She does.

When she comes out of the room, she has become emotional and upset again. My father notices right away and stands up. "What's goin on, Ana?"

Ana is sobbing. "There was a detective in there and he said that a witness said that *Nisa* set Robert on fire!" she says to my dad.

"I told him that I have not seen her and they told me to fill out a missing person's report. Raheem, he called my baby a SUSPECT!" She begins to sob loudly onto my father's shoulder.

I can't hear anything but a high-pitched noise in my ears. Nisa is an arson suspect and a runaway. Where could she be? *We don't have a hideout or nothing,* I think to myself.

It is a quiet ride home. When we pull up to our house, my dad puts the car in park and keeps the car running for a few minutes. As he gazes out of the window, he decides to ask me a question: "Jadirah, do you know where Nisa is? If you do, you need to tell me. We all love her. It's not safe for her out there alone on the street."

"I don't know where she is, Daddy."

"Do you think she tried to kill him or do you think it was an accident?"

I am silent.

"Young lady, you better speak up," my father says as he turns toward me.

I look my father courageously in the eyes: "I make my word my bond, Dad, no sir, it wasn't an accident."

"Jadirah, did you set that man on fire?" Dad asks, pushing his eyebrows together.

"No, sir, I did not," I answer with truthful confidence.

He begins to gaze at me as if he's looking into my soul. He pauses a minute. Then nods his head. "What's understood doesn't need to be said."

"Yes, sir."

"Let's go inside," he says.

The next three days are intense. Nisa's fifth grade school picture is all over the news channels. Kids at the school begin making rumors and asking me and Fatimah questions. Amirrah says that Nisa should just turn herself in.

That Wednesday night after school, Nisa shows up and taps on the kitchen window as I am doing the dishes. Startled, I look out and push the curtain aside. She waves and smiles at me and tells me, *shhh.* I rush over to the back door, wet sudsy hands and all. I am excited to see my sister friend. I quietly open the door. We keep our voices down.

"Oh my God!" I say.

"Hey J."

"Where you been?"

"Can I have some food and some juice? I'm so hungry."

"What you been eatin? Where you been stayin at?" I ask as I hand her some leftovers.

"In an empty building next to the movie theater. I've been eating thrown away popcorn for the past few days."

"The police are looking for you, I haven't said anything."

"Good, don't say nuthin—"

Before Nisa can finish her sentence, my older sister Amirrah walks in. "Nisa!" she shouts.

Nisa tries to make a run for the door and I grab her. "No!" I say.

"Lemme go!" She makes a dash for the door and runs off into the night and disappears just like that.

My mother and father hear the commotion and run into the kitchen. "What happened?"

"Was Nisa just here?"

"What did you do?"

I stand silent. Amirrah speaks up: "Nisa just ran out into the alley!"

My father sprints right out the door in his house slippers with no coat. "Raheem!" my mother cries out as he practically leaps through the back door.

"Baby girl!" he calls out. "I know you can hear me." As he slows his pace, he begins to look between the houses in the alley. "Hey sweetheart, I know you're out here. Why don't you come on out. Jeff would kill me if I let you live out in the streets." He continues to look in the bushes, as he continues: "I know you want some food. Maybe some hot tea? Come on out and come in the house…"

Just then, a glass bottle rolls in the alley. My father looks over and sees a shadow where the noise came from. He knows it's her. "Come on out, sweetheart."

Nisa walks out into the light.

"Let's get you fed and cleaned up, babygirl. Okay?" my dad says.

Our whole family is waiting and watching in the kitchen as they come back inside. My mother is in tears to see that Nisa is alive and doing okay. "Hello, sweetheart!" My mother goes to grab and hug her. Nisa smells like trash.

"Amirrah, go and run some bathwater right now," my father instructs.

"Yes, sir." Amirrah rushes up the stairs to the restroom to start the bathwater.

"Hi everybody," Nisa says quietly.

My mother releases her from the hug and sits her down. "Let me look at you, he put that bruise on your face, right?" my mother asks.

"Yes ma'am," Nisa replies.

"Let's get her a proper meal, Diane, and let's get her cleaned up. Jadirah, Fatimah, y'all go upstairs and find her a change of clean clothes and socks. Do it now, right now!" he says calmly but firmly.

"Yes, sir." We turn and follow instructions. My little brother Abdul is right behind us.

I know that my mother and father are going to try to persuade Nisa to turn herself in to the police. It's probably the best thing to do. Living on the street isn't working, obviously. Too dangerous in the hood. I pull out my most comfortable grey sweatsuit and green Cortez Nikes that she likes so much. I'm also going to give up my favorite denim jacket.

"Bathwater is ready, Mommy!" Amirrah calls out from the hall. Fatimah and I run back downstairs to the kitchen. Everyone turns to look at us. Nisa is chewing food and breathing loudly.

"What's gonna happen now?" I ask. Nisa turns to grab a sip of juice.

"Nisa has decided to turn herself over to the authorities," my father says. "Homelessness for a child with this crack mess on the street is not an option. It's not safe."

"Can't she just stay with us?" Fatimah asks.

"Honey, our family could get into trouble with the law if we did that."

Nisa wipes her mouth with the napkin. "I'm full, thank you, Auntie."

"You're welcome, baby."

"Can I have a spare toothbrush?"

"Yeah, Amirrah put everything out for you in the restroom, ok?" Nisa nods. "You leave those dirty clothes and shoes in this bag and we just gonna have everything washed clean. Okay?" Mother instructs as she hands Nisa the mesh bag.

"Yes ma'am."

Nisa goes upstairs for her bath. She seems relieved. Almost as if she wanted permission from my parents to come forward.

"Poor thing, she's exhausted," my dad says, standing up from the table.

My mother sees the concern on my face. "This is the right thing to do, Jadirah," my mother says. "We all want the best for her." My mother stands and hugs me. I still feel like this isn't fair.

"Why don't you go get my hair care basket and put two French braids in Nisa's hair when she comes out of the bath. Okay?"

"Okay, mom."

We got Nisa cleaned up, properly groomed and fed. I ask my father if I can ride with him to take Nisa to the police station. "No! The police station is serious business only." We all say goodbye and embrace. I go last and I begin to cry, I tried so hard to be tough.

"Don't cry, J," Nisa says. "I'm going to be fine." She releases me from the embrace. "Hey, thanks for the shoes, you know these are my favorite!" We giggle about it for a second.

Dad interrupts, "Okay, girls, it's time now." As they turn to leave, I think to myself, *why can't life be easier for my little friend?* Her father was killed, her mother is an addict, her brother is in the streets somewhere and she's a victim of physical abuse and rape! Why should she have to turn herself in?

I had no idea that this would be the last time I would see her for a while.

The next time I saw Nisa was in court. Robert had survived. He told the authorities that Nisa tried to kill him. It was all over the news. The charges against her: attempted murder. My father told me about an arson charge, too.

The lawyer that he got for her was an old friend of his from his Harlem days. He told us all that his strategy would be to argue self-defense due to the fact that Nisa had been sexually assaulted. He planned to plead not-guilty on her behalf. This gave the entire community hope. This wonderfully spirited, mocha-colored, tight-eyed, brilliant young girl deserved a break. I was sure that the jury would hear her plight, learn of the miscarriage of justice surrounding her father's murder by law enforcement, and would have mercy upon her.

My father and mother attended the hearings. The day of Nisa's sentencing, my father allowed me to go to court with him. He was confident that she would be acquitted of all of the charges. I knew that Grandma Faye was supposed to ride with us that day to the courthouse. She told us that she had to cancel coming with us because her spirit wouldn't be able to handle seeing Nisa as a "defendant."

We enter the courtroom and take our seats. I am filled with nervous energy and my heart is filled with regret. I look into my father's face as he glances over at me. He gives an uncertain, uneasy smile. I feel as if we are all stunned that we are even here. Please, *please* let the judge show humanity.

Ms. Ana arrives with a family friend and sits next to Mom. The lawyers arrive first, then we all sit in silence for the first few moments in the courtroom. The side door opens. The bailiff enters first, then Nisa. She has her hair pulled back in a ponytail. She wears a red and white dress with white tights and a red cardigan. It's too big for her, but it was probably donated or something.

I hear Ms. Ana gasp at the sight of her as she holds back tears. I look over at Ms. Ana to see if she is okay. My mom puts an arm around her to comfort her.

Nisa keeps her eyes to the floor as she walks to her assigned seat. She seems so steady and grown. She turns her head to the left to where we are seated. Her eyes dance around and then she looks right at me. She flashes the biggest grin I have ever seen at me. I smile back. She then notices Dad, Mom, and Ms. Ana. She blows a kiss at them and quickly turns back around to face the bench. She straightens her posture and sits quietly to await the judge.

"All rise!" the booming voice of the bailiff announces. The entire courtroom rises to their feet. "The Honorable Judge Ferguson presiding." Judge Ferguson enters the courtroom through a side door. He is an older white man with grey hair and a medium build. He is wearing a frown and I don't have a good feeling about him.

"You may all be seated," Ferguson announces to the court. The prosecutor rises to give the opening address. Words are thrown around for about fifteen minutes. I'm in and out of listening because I don't really understand what any of it means. All I hear is, "Your honor, the plaintiff accuses," "this young lady is responsible for damages, other homes could have burned!" "Self-defense," "Committed a crime," "No proof," "Let us close this case," "Guilty!" "Not guilty!"

The judge's ruling is in. The judge asks Nisa if she has anything she'd like to say before he announces his decision. "Do you have anything to say for yourself, young lady?"

Nisa clears her throat and says, "Yes, your honor." She stands and pulls out a small piece of paper with words written on it. "I would like the court to know that I understood what I did. I acted alone and I know that you all don't accept a young lady doing what I did. You think that I am a bad person and you think I should go to jail. I do not regret what I did." The courtroom gasps at the lack of Nisa's remorse. "I was being drugged and raped. I feel that I was in the right in trying to take that horrible person off of this earth. I do not deserve to go to jail. I should be at school. Thank you," she says confidently. As she takes her seat, she folds the small piece of paper and places it in her cardigan pocket.

The judge wants to make a statement: "Young lady, I admire your honesty. I am aware of the many tragedies that have occurred in your very short thirteen years. What you did is very much illegal and I find your lack of remorse insulting to my court. You speak with such full assurance and are excessively bold about what you have done here."

Nisa gazes at him emotionless, almost impatient, as if she's ready to get on with it.

"I hereby sentence Nisa Edwards to two and a half years at Philadelphia Juvenile Detention Center, no parole!" He bangs his gavel and stands up quickly.

The courtroom is filled with members of the community that become outraged with the verdict. Ms. Ana is crying hysterically. I well up with tears as handcuffs are placed upon my best friend's small wrists. She turns around through the commotion of the crowd to look for my dad. She locks eyes with him and mouths, "I'll be fine," and then looks at me, gives a slight smirk and nods. Not in an arrogant way but in a realistic, secure way. Suddenly, I don't feel so sad about the verdict. She's going to be fine. She is capable of doing this time.

How is this little girl so tough? She is on her way to jail with handcuffs on and brimming with confidence at the same time. What valor, she didn't cry! I know that she'll be able to handle herself.

"I'm really going to miss her," I say to my father.

"Let's go home," he says.

My father took me to visit Nisa once a month for two and a half years. He kept his word. I will always appreciate how my father is about giving his word. He always says, "Your word is your bond!" Ms. Ana moved back to New York to stay with her cousins. My mother and father made arrangements for Nisa to come and live with our family once her time was served.

"When she gets here with us, no more poor decisions, no more hard luck," my father said to the whole family before Nisa came to live with us. I was allowed to ride with Mom and Dad to pick up Nisa from the detention center. I felt anxious and excited at the exact same time. I could hear my heart beating when we pulled into the parking lot.

When we get into the building, my mother asks me, "How are you feeling, baby?"

"Kinda nervous but excited, too," I reply.

"She'll be fine, she's with us now," my father says, assuring me.

We walk down the hall and my mother and I sit in the waiting area while Dad fills out the paperwork for processing. It is more comfortable for Dad to stand while we await Nisa's arrival. We wait for about ten minutes in complete silence. Then we hear a loud thud, the sound of a heavy door closing and a sharp squeak of metal door hinges. My mother stands up and smiles, "Here she is!"

I stand up and notice how tall she is and how she managed to stuff her now sixteen-year-old self back into my old comfy grey sweatsuit, denim jacket and green Cortez Nikes with the white swoosh on the sides. I begin to smile as she walks down the hall toward us behind all of that glass.

There is a security officer escorting her. My mother notices a bandage above her left eye. "Oh no, I wonder what happened," Mom murmurs under her breath.

Nisa smiles and gives a quick wave to us as she gathers her belongings and signs some paperwork. She stands at the door with the window and we hear a loud buzz. Then a click. She opens the door and runs straight to me first. She embraces me tightly and begins to chuckle with delight. "Hey Jay!" she says. Her voice is husky now. She sounds like those girls in the hood who like to fight.

"Hey, Nisa, we missed you!"

She releases from the hug, then hugs my mother next, then Dad. "Look at you…" My dad holds her face and looks into Nisa's eyes. "Our little survivor!"

The drive home is spirited and optimistic. It takes a little adjusting to hear this new raspy Philly accent of hers. My dad jokes, "Nisa, you sound like those ladies from back in the day that could sing real good!" That moment, Nisa jokingly starts to sing, "The Greatest Love of All," by Whitney Houston. Mom, Dad and I erupt in laughter. Her sense of humor is still intact.

I'm in awe of the fortitude that remained with her after this whole ordeal. Once we all calm ourselves of the laughter, my mother asks us what dinner should be for tonight. Of course, Mother's intent is to engage Nisa in talking about her desire for her first home-cooked meal, fresh out of jail.

"Fried fish, mac n' cheese and some greens! I've been dreaming about some fried fish with hot sauce!" Nisa blurts out.

"Ohh that gets my vote! Except I want some yellow rice instead of mac n cheese," my Father chimes in.

As my father and Nisa chat about supper plans, I'm observing her. I'm looking for sadness or anger, maybe even disappointment. I don't see any brokenness in her spirit. She isn't a phony, so I can tell that she's not pretending to be fine.

"It was terrible food in Juvie," Nisa announces as the car falls silent from the chatter.

"Well, baby, you don't have to worry about that place ever again. What happened to your face?" my mother asks curiously.

Nisa pauses for a moment before she answers, "I got into it with some girls."

"Over what, honey?"

"Nothin really, she was just jealous that I was getting out, that's all," Nisa folds her arms and raises her eyebrows. She then turns her eyes to look out of the car window. She slowly begins to rock back and forth. She clearly does not want to talk about the altercation.

"Let's put the radio on, y'all," suggests my Father to rid us of the awkward silence. The rest of the ride home seems to pass quickly, once the music is on.

She orders herself to relax a bit. Her body language becomes less tense once we get back to the old stomping grounds in the neighborhood. Nisa's face lights up as she quietly observes the changes around town. Suddenly her face takes on a frown. "What did they do to the candy store?" Nisa asks.

"Some Chinese man bought it. They're turning it into a beauty supply store," Dad announces as he slows the driving to a stop at the red light. Nisa has no response to the new information.

"We are going to take you shopping for clothes later on," Mom says, hoping to cheer her up.

Nisa's face lights up as she smiles. "Thank you!" she replies. Mother smiles back and nods.

We arrive home and Amirrah has started preparing the food for dinner. My little brother Abdul is playing Nintendo on the good TV in the living room.

"We're home!" Dad announces.

Amirrah comes out of the kitchen. "Hey now, welcome back!" she says as she embraces Nisa.

Mom starts toward the kitchen. "Did you take the fish out of the freezer?" she asks Amirrah.

"Yes ma'am."

"Nisa, you're back!" little Abdul says, giving Nisa a little side hug.

"You call that a hug? Give me a big hug and a big ol' kiss." Nisa kisses Abdul on the cheek and he frowns his face up with disgust.

"Eww, stop it!" he says, wiping the kiss from his face.

Dad hangs his coat and starts toward the stereo.

"It's been a long time coming, time to celebrate and I know just the song." Dad pops an Earth, Wind and Fire tape in and cues it to their magical tune, "Fantasy." "Yeah!" he says as the first few notes begin.

"Turn that one up, Raheem, you know I can't hardly hear in the kitchen!" Mom demands. Dad grabs his guitar to play along to one of our family's favorite songs. Even Amirrah begins to dance. She's typically the reserved one.

My father has always encouraged us to dance to music or go on a walk if things are very good, very bad, uncertain, or to simply clear your head. He would also encourage us to pray in those same situations. I am dancing and singing along with my family and I notice Nisa's energy. She seems so happy and free! Comfortable and uninhibited.

After dinner, Mom allows me and Fatimah to go on a short walk with Nisa before we take off for the shopping center. As we walk, we see well-wishers and neighbors speaking to Nisa with words of encouragement. "Hey baby!" "Welcome back!" "They can't keep a real one down!" "Your daddy is smiling down on you, sugar!"

"You are like a famous person out here in North Philly, Nisa!" Fatimah says excitedly at all of the attention. We all chuckle a bit.

"Wait till everybody catch me in my new gear! I wanna get some FUBU! Everybody inside was talking about getting some Fubu or Cross Colors!" Nisa says.

"What was it like in there?" I ask.

"What… jail?"

"Yeah, what did you do on a day-to-day?"

Nisa just stays silent for a few steps then says, "I survived, you just stay out the way."

"Yeah, I get that but I mean like…"

Nisa interrupts. "Okay, I don't like talking about jail. No disrespect, all straight, all love. I'm out now and I ain't going back. Okay? Sorry… but…" She's shaking her head and her voice trails off.

"No, it's cool," I say.

"We better head back home, Mommy probably ready to go," Fatimah adds.

As we started to walk home, all I could think about was how calm and authoritative Nisa's voice was when she just checked me about jail. It was like talking to a real adult! I suppose her circumstances in there forced her to mature in ways that I hadn't thought about.

She set boundaries early on. I have to admit, my respect for Nisa grew when I saw her protect me from all the trouble.

FIVE

Visions

Only Mama, Fatimah and Nisa know about the cancer. I don't want anyone treating me with pity. Like a cripple or someone that is needy. No investigation. No right to speak. I don't talk about it. I don't focus on it. If I focus on this problem, this problem will get bigger.

I've been doing hair since I was sixteen years old. I've never done anything else. After years of standing over press and curl smoke, hairspray, oil sheen spray, spritz, perm fumes and, not to mention, surviving the Brazilian blowout craze, I managed to hang on by the skin of my teeth. Just barely.

I have lung cancer and severe carpal tunnel in my right wrist from all of the flat-ironing and braiding. My courage will not fail. I will not disappoint myself and I damn sure still have fire from within telling me to press on! I've had to always conform when it comes to me and my business. I plan to set my own rules!

I arrive early to the salon to prepare for my first client, Imani. A beautiful sorority lady who just made partner at the law firm where she works. She's also the best-dressed woman I've known, next to Nisa. She is a successful entrepreneur, she's on the youth ministry team at her church, and she is the most annoying narcissist that I've ever met. She wants a man but can't keep one. Her stark and lonely life has made her a bitter, corporate sistah. Since the ladies at the salon have dubbed her "The Mean Lady," I no longer service her during normal business hours. She actually told a client who was agnostic that she was going to burn in hell. I can't stand her attitude or her slick remarks, but she tips so damn well. I'll tolerate it… for now.

I enter Jay's Beauty Salon and turn the lights on. A sense of challenge comes over me. The decisions that I've been making lately are giving me a feeling of independence. Maybe the years of quiet compliance with Carlos have given me the fuel I need to take a stand.

I can't believe I sold my shop! I'll tell Tina and Lelah later, but for now… music. I decide on Stevie Wonder this early, holy-feeling morning. "Superwoman" is my selection.

It has been a blessing to work in here. To create jobs, to extend positivity in the community. I understand this community and so does Nisa. I'll see to it that nothing changes but I'm sure she'll remodel the entire space.

I sit for about a half hour listening to "Songs in the Key of Life" by Stevie Wonder. I fall into a daydream of what my plans for my family should have been. "Ordinary Pain" comes on as I stare out the window, as I await the arrival of Imani. I begin to sing along. I understand every single message and begin to reflect. I well up with tears as I re-examine some of my life choices. I quickly turn to some Robert Glasper tunes to change the melancholy mood that I am about to place myself in. I have to put my mind back into work mode.

"What could I have done differently?" I ask myself. I can only wonder. I never gave myself a chance. I sigh and tell myself, "Ok, pull yourself together and get ready." I will develop an idea to put my family on track. But for now… I am tasked with two clients to service this morning and I will do just that. I look out the window and notice Imani pulling up in her fire-engine red, brand new E-Class 350 Mercedes. "Okay, here we go…" I say aloud before she approaches the door with her laptop case, book bag and Hermes handbag. I raise my eyebrows, place a polite tight-lipped smile across my face in an attempt to appear delighted to see her. I wave quickly when she notices me through the glass door. I unlock and open the door. Her hands are full and it's the least I can do. I mean, she's a pain, but she is a loyal client, after all. I keep her sew-in looking right!

"Good morning!" I say cheerfully. She smells like Versace bright crystal perfume.

"Good morning, Jadirah! How have you been?" Imani says, entering the salon. I lock the door back. "Ohh, that candle smells great! Is it vanilla?"

"Yes it is."

"I can't believe how chilly it is this morning," Imani stops to look around and notices a balloon arrangement left over from last night from the Friday group. "What's the occasion? What's the balloons for?" Imani widens her eyes and looks directly at my face.

"Oh, the girls wanted to do something nice for my birthday and these balloons are here from yesterday."

"Oh okay, balloons for a grown woman's birthday, wow!" she says in a condescending tone. "I guess it's the thought that counts. How cute is that?" She stiffens and clasps her hands together as I draw away to study her face.

"It feels nice to be loved," I reply to the shady remarks that Imani seems to be in the mood for.

"Yeah, yeah, if I would have known it was your birthday, I would have sent roses," she says in a friendly high-pitched phony valley-girl voice. "Grown women should be getting roses. Balloons are cool, you know, for kids, but to each his own."

I decide to end the chat before I react. "Are you getting a wash and style today?"

"Yes, I want it set on rollers for lots of body."

"Okay, you can come back to the first bowl once you get all settled."

We are typically quiet during our time together for the appointment. I'm fine with that. She usually texts and responds to emails while I shampoo and condition her luxurious sew-in weave and leave out. After the shampoo service is finished we head on over to my workstation to begin the roller set.

I see that I've missed a call and it was Dr. Heinz. I begin wondering what it was that she called about. She usually texts. As I begin to work on Imani's set, I wonder if Imani is in the mood for any small talk. I notice her typing away on her laptop and decide to put a test question out there to see if she feels like a little girl-talk or if it's business as usual. "Do you have a busy day today?" I ask.

"Yes," she replies rapidly, typing with a focused energy. She clearly doesn't want to be bothered with any talk that won't make her money or lift her status.

After I finish the roller set and get Imani under the hood dryer, I decide to call Dr. Heinz back. I make the call and she answers on the second ring. "Hello?"

"Hello, Dr. Heinz! Good morning!" I say.

"Jadirah! Did you get my message?"

"I haven't listened to my voicemail, I just saw that I missed your call."

"Oh, okay, I just wanted to ask if I could come in a little earlier this morning instead of nine o'clock?"

"Sure, that's no problem, Dr. Heinz."

"Okay, I'm going to stop for a coffee. Did you want anything?"

"I'm good, thanks; see ya soon!" I end the call. I realize that I will not be finished with Imani's service when Dr. Heinz arrives for her twist set. I believe that the peaceful disposition of Dr. Heinz will shift any aggressive energies that Imani would emit.

Dr. Heinz is a client that I look forward to seeing. She always smells like eucalyptus and lavender oils with a touch of lemongrass. She's a psychologist, a peripatetic with five homes in the United States, a real estate investor and a retired superintendent of the local school district. She spends her summer vacation in Ghana every year and is the most humble intellectual you could ever meet. Never pretentious, most people aren't even aware that she's a doctor. She's observant and awake, never quick to judge. When she goes on a rant about anything, she commands the shop's attention with finesse, she's so articulate and eloquent. She typically requests a two-strand twist set on her curly mid-back tresses.

Dr. Heinz arrives and I open the door. "Good morning, little sister!" she says with her Georgia drawl.

"Dr. Heinz! Good morning to you!" I reach for a hug. We embrace. "How have you been?"

"I should be asking you that, Jadirah."

"I have been doing okay."

We pull away from the embrace, she holds my hands and looks into my eyes. "Of course, did you get some time off?" she says in a calm, nurturing voice.

"I did!"

She nods with a gentle smile. Her eyes dance around my face, observing my scars from the fall on the right side of my face. "Well, let me hang my jacket."

"What style did you want to have done today?"

"The twists will be fine, my dear. It's like having two styles in one," she says, hanging her jacket in the waiting area.

I absolutely adore this lady. She's dressed in black sweat pants, black well-worn New Balance sneakers, a white T-shirt that says "Las Vegas" on it, a black duster, tiny ruby earrings, colorful Kenyan beaded bracelets on one wrist and silver bangles on the other. She's the only millionaire that I've met who comes into the hood on a regular basis and blends in. She's a boss and a revolutionary. A prideful, cultured woman. She is my mentor. She gave me the pep talk to motivate me to open my own business.

As we start at the shampoo bowl, she begins pulling apart her two French braids. "I can help you with that," I say to her.

"I meant to take it down in the car on my way over here…"

"It's no problem, I got you." As I start the shampooing process, I notice that Imani's hood dryer has turned off. I know that the foundation braided base and thread of the weave is not fully dried yet. I need to go and restart it after I rinse Dr. Heinz's first shampoo. "Excuse me Dr. Heinz, I'll be right back."

"Okay."

As I'm walking to Imani's dryer, she decides to state the obvious. "My dryer cut off," she says as she types on her MacBook.

"No worries, I'll just restart it." I set her dryer to forty-five minutes on the timer. That's about how long it'll take me to twist Dr. Heinz's curly tresses.

As I walk back to the shampoo area to finish, Dr. Heinz asks a question. "Is the young lady that does pedicures coming in today?"

"Yes ma'am, she is. Did you want an appointment?"

"Yeah, I'd like to set one up for next Saturday, actually. I haven't had one all winter and I'm embarrassed to say that I've neglected my poor feet these past few months."

"I'm sure she has openings, Dr. Heinz. She usually comes in on Saturdays between 10:30 and 11:00 a.m. Okay, we can head over to the first chair," I instruct as we end the shampoo service.

"Well I certainly hope that she doesn't judge me when she pulls my socks off to submerge my feet in the bowl. I've failed to properly care for my poor tired feet, because I've been so busy," Dr. Heinz says as she sits down in the styling chair.

I begin to towel dry and detangle her silver and dark brown tresses. "Yeah, I'm just the same, I keep my nails done, though. Everyone can see my nails, everyone does not get a chance to see my feet. I should probably book an appointment too!" I say jokingly.

Dr. Heinz chuckles. I begin to section her hair to start the twist. "Jadirah, do you ever sometimes wonder why we do that as black women? Neglect? Why we struggle to make time for self-care or even take time for privacy where one retires to adequately care for themselves, meditate, get a massage, and things like that?"

"I know for me, it's finding the time. Between the shop and dealing with the children and all of their activities, I'm always on the go or working."

"So are white women, so are Middle Eastern women and everyone else," she says in her teaching tone of voice. I can tell she's in the mood to teach this morning. "Black women in America are used to being neglected. We sometimes expect to be forgotten and ignored. We are simply accustomed to inadequate care, whether it be medical, dental, in relationships… especially in relationships. Many sistahs that I've known believe that it is their responsibility to stay in godforsaken relationships to prove they are ride or die."

I can tell that Dr. Heinz did not come to play this morning. Clearly, she saw the video of me on social media and she has come in earlier than usual to tell me what's on her mind in a classy discreet manner, as she always does. "I divorced my husband when I was thirty-nine years old. I wanted to grow and he was in my way. The marriage became difficult because he had so much mental garbage, it jeopardized our stability and we couldn't work together in clarity. Poor thing, he wanted to lead and just didn't know how to!" She shakes her head and sighs as she pauses a moment. "Movement does not mean rejection. It only means that we want to broaden our scope. We owe it to ourselves in a space that will provide and support our vision for our life!"

"I know that's right, Dr. Heinz," I reply, knowing for certain that she's speaking about Carlos and I and the volatile state of our marriage. She's on a roll and I'm eager to listen, eager to be receptive of the message she has come to share with me.

"Have you ever watched the History Channel and watched their program on ghost towns in the wild west?" she asks.

"Yes, I've seen a few."

"You ever wonder what those towns *used* to be like before they were abandoned? Or what attracted groups of people to those towns, whether it be a rumor of a gold rush or free land, the promise of a good railway job, and things like that. Promise! Promise of a good life, promise of starting a family. Thriving! Living good, keeping up a good appearance. And then to see a town with so much opportunity and promise and assurance that a particular thing will be! Would later turn up dry and desolate. Deserted of people and in a state of dismal emptiness. I am moved to believe that we, as humans, have the ability to recover spiritually and emotionally from neglect and emptiness, you know?"

"Yes, definitely."

We are silent for a moment. I notice that Imani is listening quietly to Dr. Heinz as her eyes draw up to us a few times as she takes breaks from typing.

"You know a great quote I used to say to my staff that I loved was, *You can't have what you want until you want what you have.* I forgot who said it but it stayed with me!" she laughs.

"We have to take care, we are worthy! We cannot afford to forget ourselves. We must know what to do as women. And we need a nudge sometimes to get us back on track. A REALITY CHECK. So when something happens to us, remember things just don't happen, they happen as they should, in the right order, and it may be uncomfortable. Our job as women is to understand what is happening. Okay? And to know that we are going to handle our business."

"Yes, definitely taking notes this morning, Dr. Heinz. You are a whole sensei on my life this morning!"

We erupt in laughter as I prepare to finish her damp twist around her edges and crown. What a blessing she brought through her this morning. I understand all of her examples and with so much meaning!

I place Dr. Heinz under a preheated hood dryer. I then go to check on Imani. "Just about ten more minutes, okay?" I inform Imani of the time left.

"Okay that's fine. May I have a little water? It's so hot under here," Imani says, wrinkling her nose.

"Sure, I'll be right back."

As I get Imani's water, I begin to ponder about the words that Dr. Heinz used. Neglect, adequate care, forgotten, ignored, mental garbage, stability, movement, rejection, promise! Dr. Heinz has always been eloquent. She always thinks before she speaks so that no one misunderstands her. She spoke directly to my situation, directly to my soul.

"Here you go, Imani, almost dry!" I say, placing the disposable plastic cup beside her on the side table.

"Okay, thanks," she says, not looking up from her laptop.

I go to check my phone and notice that I have three text messages. One from my sister, Fatimah, and the other two from clients trying to get an appointment for today. I text the clients back immediately to let them know that I'm close to being done for today and I forward Tina's number to them.

That way they can ask if she has any openings. I decide not to text my sister back. I prefer to call her.

I look through social media for a few minutes and I come across my video on a black culture page and shake my head. I put my phone down and rub my face. I'm curious about what the community feels. I pick my phone up and I go down into the comments. The question asked is: *Why do we as a community fail to stick to a budget?* The comments hurt, some are funny, some are sad, some are comforting and some are just emojis. I put my phone down and I decide to finish Imani's hair. As I put the finishing touches on Imani's styling service, she becomes curious about Dr. Heinz.

"Jadirah, who is the lady under the dryer?" she asks me in a hushed tone of voice.

"That's Dr. Josephine Heinz," I reply.

"Is she a medical doctor or…"

"She's a psychologist, she received her Doctorate of Education as well."

"Oh that's quite impressive, I overheard you all's conversation and she's really deep!"

"Yeah, she'll get deep if she feels moved to. She's typically kinda quiet and observant."

"Hmmm," Imani replies as she falls into an introspective silence for the rest of the appointment.

I style and blend her leave-out and lay her edges to the heavens. I spray the finishing sheen spray and hand her the mirror.

"Perfect every time!" she says cheerfully, pleased as she hands me the mirror back. "Okay, so I'm already scheduled for my next appointment and I already sent today's payment."

"Yes, thanks, I received it."

"So we're all set? Thank you so much! You ladies have a good one," Imani says as she gathers her things and hurries out of the salon.

"Bye, have a good one!" I reply.

"Take care," says Dr. Heinz. We watch Imani leave and Dr. Heinz has a question. "Okay, may I please come out of this dryer?" she says humorously.

"Sure, come on out of there. Come on over, I just need to put a little oil on your scalp and we're all set."

Dr. Heinz gets settled into the styling chair. "Jadirah, may I pull this off? I feel a hot flash coming through," she refers to the comb-out cape.

"Sure, that's fine! Get comfortable."

She hands me the comb-out cape and I toss it onto the empty station next to mine. "So Jadirah, how are the boys, how is my little Ava?"

"The children are fine, resilient and bright as ever. The older two boys struggled a bit when, you know, things went left last week."

"They have every right to be upset, you are their mother," Dr. Heinz says in a very firm tone. I am silent. I continue on with the service. "Jadirah, may I ask you a personal question, lil sis?"

"Sure you can, anything you want!"

"Okay. What is your vision for your family?"

I pause. "I ummm, I've never been asked that question before."

"Have you ever thought about or planned your future with Carlos?"

I clear my throat. "I'm embarrassed to say, well, no. We've ahh… I don't know, just live and maintain."

"So no five-year plan or ten-year plan?"

"We had a retirement plan, we had to cash it out though, for an emergency."

"Do you all have a financial advisor?"

"We had one. I usually manage my income, the salon expenses, and make sure we don't ever do a joint account." We laugh together momentarily. "Dr. Heinz, I know I'm not a financial planner, my instinct is to save for when trouble comes, after all, I'm just a college drop-out hairdresser," I say jokingly.

Dr. Heinz turns around slowly to face me and grabs my hands. I chuckle nervously. She has a very serious look upon her face. "My dear little sister, do not ever say things like that. Don't do that to yourself, 'Just a hairdresser.' Do you know that hairstylists, barbers and groomers held high ranks and respect in certain ancient African civilizations? In ancient Egypt alone, style was an artistic representation of wealth, class and social status in society. If you look in the mirror and your hair is a mess, you don't feel so good about yourself. When you go and get a fresh 'do,' your whole frequency changes when you see your appearance! We need our stylists and tastemakers to keep us on our square. It's Western culture that makes our creators feel less than! And never forget that! You are a creative vessel, okay, and your gift is a blessing!"

"You got it, dang, I guess you done told me!"

We laugh it out. Dr. Heinz stands and we embrace. "Alright, if you need me for anything, call me. Jadirah, I'm serious."

"You got it! It was so good to see you today."

Dr. Heinz smiles and grabs her jacket, she never looks at her hair in the mirror after I've completed her service. She says goodbye and goes on about her day. I've always admired the way she carries herself.

Her questions about me planning my future have me in a state of wonder. I don't feel pressured into a vision, I feel motivated. Motivated to succeed. My vision is my success. I must confess, my fears and concerns will no longer hold me back from creating a vision to follow.

SIX

Do It Now

Why in the hell don't these ignorant knee-grows put the damn shopping carts where they're supposed to go!" I murmur to myself as I move two shopping carts at the ghetto supermarket parking lot out of the available parking space so that I may shop for groceries for dinner tonight. I put the carts with the rest of the carts in the cart space. Frustrated, I hop back into my car, start it and back into the parking space carefully. I park, turn my car off, and begin to gather my things to get out of the car and get started shopping. I look out over the dashboard and notice a bum watching me. I've seen him before and he's a harmless drunk. I take out a dollar bill just for him, exit and lock my car.

"Aww man, Ms. Lady, how ya doin? Could you spare some change please, I'm short on my bus fare," he asks while reeking of whiskey and cigarette smoke. He is dusty and raggedy, I feel pity for him and hand him the dollar bill.

"Here you go, take care."

"Aww thanks, pretty lady. Thank ya!" he replies.

I simply nod and head into the store. I'm grabbing a shopping basket when Nisa calls from her primary cell-phone number. I am excited to answer. I take my basket and head over to the produce section of the supermarket; at this location, it's usually pretty empty, with only a few elders shopping. The aisles with the processed foods and the meat are always more heavily populated.

I answer the call: "Hey sis!"

"Hey beautiful! Where are you? You at the shop?" Nisa asks.

"No, I'm at the store, I just left the shop. I needed to pick up a few things for dinner."

"Okay cool, I am in the city out and about with Tony. We shall see you in a few hours, sis."

"Okay good, I'm so excited."

"Okay, love, love."

"Love," I end the call. Smiling, I decide to text Fatimah back. She wants to know if I plan on attending Dad's show tonight. I text her that I'm not sure yet and that we plan on having dinner guests.

"Excuse me, baby," I hear a sweet southern accent in a voice that sounds like my Grandma Robinson. I quickly turn around to see what's going on.

"Yes ma'am?"

"You blockin' the greens, baby," the sweet elder says with a chuckle.

"Oh, well, let me move out your way!" I say in a cheerful, friendly manner as I step aside.

"You didn't have to hop out da way, sugar, I just needed you to scoot a lil bit so I can pick out my greens."

"Okay, okay, sorry about that ma'am, you have a blessed one."

"Okay sweetheart, you too."

As I move on with my shopping, I realize that I should move quickly so that I'll have enough time to prepare everything without rushing. I then remember that only Ava, David and Ezekiel are at home. I think to call Isaiah to see if he and Carlos are finished at the barber shop.

Isaiah picks up on the first ring. "'Sup Mom?"

"Hey baby, how you doin?"

"Doing good, we just got finished at the barber shop. Huh… oh okay. Dad wants me to put it on speaker, Mom."

I roll my eyes and simply say, "Okay."

"Hey, baby, me and 'Saiah just finished at the barbershop and we're heading home now. Where are you?"

"I'm at the store. Hey, will you have the children clean the house real good? We might have…"

I hesitate for a moment. I can't tell Carlos that Nisa is coming over for dinner. The last time I told him that she was stopping by for a visit, it was a paparazzi disaster!

I continue, "… we might have family stopping by for dinner later on."

"Oh, okay, well I'm just going to be dropping Isaiah off at home and he can tell 'em, cause I gotta go and pick up Ronnie and we're going down to the rec center for basketball."

Now I usually get upset at this kind of surprise, spur-of-the-moment, thoughtless way that my poor husband does things. But today, it's perfect! "Okay, that's fine. Isaiah? Did you hear all of that? Clean the house, get the sibs to help and spend most of the time on the kitchen and guest bathroom. Okay?"

"Okay Mom, I got you."

"I know you do. Love you! See you later," I end the call. I know that I can count on my son. He is about his word.

I check off every item on my shopping list and I am done! After an uneventful self-checkout, I am completely finished with the grocery store for today. I check the time on my cell-phone and it reads 1:07 p.m., and just as I check the time I get a call from Isaiah's phone. I frown my face with concern. I worry that something is wrong. "Isaiah? Hello?"

"Mommy, it's Ava!"

"Hey baby, what's wrong?"

"Someone just pulled up to the house in a fancy car," Ava says.

"Mom, it's a Bentley!" Ezekiel says from the background.

"Oh my God! Mom! It's Auntie Nisa! She's got a tall man with locs helping her out of the car!" Ava says excitedly.

I hear the boys clamoring in the background and, although I'm surprised, concerned, and excited all at once, I remember the rules. "Okay Ava, I was not expecting her this early. Have the boys put all smart devices in the wicker basket by the front door."

"Okay, they're doing it now, I have you on speaker, Mommy. Wow, she looks so pretty! Her hair is pulled up in a long ponytail, she has on a white jacket with fur around the collar, some shattered jeans and the coldest green suede boots I've ever seen, Mom! You should see her shades!"

I smile at the description of my fly-ass sister friend. Green is her favorite color, it has been for some time now. I suddenly think of the green Cortez Nikes that I had that she loved. I think of how far she has come since those rough times. North Philly's proud success story. The fashion and entertainment mogul has arrived on the humble—well, kind of. The Bentley is certainly not self-effacing.

"Ava, don't tell anyone that she is here. Okay?"

"Yes ma'am."

"Okay, put Isaiah on the phone."

"Hello Mom?"

"Isaiah? Look, did y'all clean the house real good?"

"Yes ma'am."

"Okay, let Nisa and Tony in the house and don't tell anyone that they're here. Not even your Dad. Okay?"

"Yes ma'am."

"Okay, bye." I end the call and rush to my car to pop the trunk to arrange the groceries inside. I finish up and hop into the driver's seat, strap on my seat belt and head home.

Nisa hadn't meant to be away for so long, but my chaotic circumstances put a sense of urgency in her that I haven't seen in a while. We have each other's back. She is here to check on me and my children. She's not here to talk about her new reality show or her clothing collaboration with Louie Brossard, or any celebrity gossip about her and Jakka! For the first time in my own tragedy, I feel a sense of contentment and safety, knowing that my very best friend is here to show support. I'm shocked that she has arrived so early.

I pull up to the front of my house and there is a white Bentley Bentayga parked outside of my house. I smile and shake my head. She has to ride in style. As I approach the front door, I feel an impatience growing inside of me. I sit the grocery bags on the porch. I feel anxious but I also feel joy. I wonder if she'll remember our greeting from back in the day when we were heavy into fresh Hip Hop and new in the entertainment business. I chuckle as I grab the keys to open the door. Quietly opening the front door, I hear laughter and conversation in the kitchen. I decide to sneak up on everyone.

"Yo Nisa Nis!!" I begin to rap.

"Alright, okay," she replies with a grin.

"How you feel?"

"Feelin great!"

"What you want?"

"I wanna do it to death, wussup with you?"

"You know my steez."

"True indeed."

"Say it loud."

"Black and proud!"

We say together as always, "Ain't no time to hesitate at the gate, do it now!"

"Ahh!" Nisa shouts in delight as I reach for a hug and we embrace with laughter and invincible vibes. She pulls me back to take a look at me, "Hey beautiful!"

"Hey girl!" I begin to crack up laughing. "Why are y'all here so early? Hey Tony!" I reach to give Tony a hug.

"How are you, Jadirah?" Tony asks.

"Doing good, surprised! Have the children been taking care of you all?"

"Oh these babies have been wonderful! I can't believe how tall Isaiah and Zeek are now!" Tony settles back and gets comfortable.

They have been snacking on a pretzel mix that the children prepared for them. I'm beside myself with gratitude. I instruct the boys to go out onto the porch to fetch the groceries as I hang my jacket and pre-heat the oven, and everyone makes small talk. I feel so good in this moment, so good that I decide to put on some 90's R&B to get the vibe going. I have to admit, I don't feel grief, fear or pain in this moment. It feels good, because that's what I've felt all week.

SEVEN

Survival of the Fittest

So Zeek! I heard you started a rap group at school," Nisa blurts out at Ezekiel while holding David hostage on her lap in the kitchen nook.

"Yep! It's gon' be hot, too!" Ezekiel responds.

"So what's the name of your group?" Tony asks curiously.

"Drip Gang Top!" Ava blurts out excitedly.

"Oh okay, so what do y'all rap about? What's the lyrical content like?" Tony asks.

"I'll send you the link and you can check us out on YouTube," Ezekiel says, going to grab his phone.

"No, no, send it later!" I instruct, checking on the progress of the rice I'm cooking. "No phones right now, baby. Okay?"

"Okay, Mom," Ezekiel replies.

"Alright, so lemme ask you a question. Who are your top three emcees excluding Hov, Big and Nas?" Tony asks Ezekiel, narrowing his eyes.

"Okay so… Imma go with Kendrick, J. Cole and Drake," Ezekiel states.

"Okay not bad," Tony says, nodding with approval. "Who you got for your top three groups?"

"I got Migos, Tribe, and WuTang and the Lox!"

"No, you can't do that, that's four, Zeek!" Nisa says in laughter.

"I can't choose three groups," Ezekiel says, laughing slightly.

"You shoulda said Drip Gang Top first!" Nisa adds. "Always include yourselves!"

"Okay, so let me switch it up. Do you have a top three Hip Hop duo list?" Tony asks.

"Oh wow…umm," Ezekiel begins to think as he rubs all five chin hairs on his face. He then raises his eyebrows as if he's figured it out. "I got it! Outkast, Mob Deep and Black Star!"

"Oh yeah, that sounds like your mom's list right there!" Nisa says cheerfully.

"I know, right!" I laugh as I prepare the salmon patties.

"Now I got one, I got one! Who are your top three female emcees?" Nisa asks as she sits back and folds her arms in the dining chair with a smirk across her face.

"Oh okay, I got you. I like Rhapsody, she got flow, Lauryn Hill and Eve!" Ezekiel responds with a smile.

"Whaaat?" Tony says shocked. "I just knew that you were going to say, Nikki, Remi and Cardi or something along those lines." Tony smiles as if he knows what the young kids like.

"I know his mama done influenced that list and you better had said Eve, that's Philly's finest, right there!" Nisa smiles.

"And you know it! Classic Hip Hop for these babies all day!" I say, popping a grape into my mouth as I continue to prepare dinner.

"You know your mom used to rap back in the day with me and Auntie Fatimah when we were just kids," Nisa states, looking in my direction.

"We used to make up dance routines to our lil songs," I respond.

"Sure did! Remember the talent show?"

"Oh God. How could I forget!"

"Look y'all, before all of this social media and everything like that, all the kids in the neighborhood would make dance routines to their favorite songs," Nisa says to the children.

"We did Miss Sidlow's annual talent show with some original music that we had done and we did good but no one knew the song, so we lost!" I say.

"Yeah, and we never tried to do any more talent contests after that! For some reason it just never seemed to work out. It was actually around that time period that your mom's clientele started to grow and my interest in fashion really started to drive me to learn more."

"That's right! My dad had a musician buddy he used to work with hook me up to braid Jakeem's hair for his music video shoot. His regular braider got sick and I got my chance and… I took Nisa with me. She kinda, I don't know, it just happened that she began styling the video models!"

"Wow, for real!?" says an intrigued Ava.

"Isn't Jakeem a preacher or minister now?" asks a curious Isaiah.

"He is! I want to say an Israelite movement minister or something like that, but back in the day he was a pistol!" says Nisa. "He was the hottest singer out!"

"And you know that's right, groupies were everywhere at that video shoot," I add.

"That was the start of it. Your mom did Jakeem's hair and that braid style was the catalyst for both of our careers. I mean your mom, Jadirah, started receiving calls from pro ball players, entertainers, fashion models, you name it! And I would be right there styling everyone!" Nisa says excitedly.

"We were so young while all of this was going on, just kids, I think we were sixteen and doin' it."

"Yes we were, ambitious!"

"And driven. Dad got us an agent to book our gigs and everything," I add, frying the salmon patties.

"Yeah we had it going on!" Nisa adds, standing from her chair.

"Auntie Nisa, my mom has a picture taken with you and you had a crimped ponytail and a swoop bang. Now when was that picture taken?" Ava asks.

"Oh wow, honey. I was wondering what happened to my picture. I guess the picture thief strikes again, Jadirah?" Nisa responds, looking in my direction.

Ezekiel darts out of the room. I pretend I don't hear her because I am guilty of taking pictures from loved ones. It's kind of an inside joke.

"Uhh… Jadirah?" says Nisa.

"Huh? I don't know what you talkin about, I'm busy over here cooking dinner."

"Auntie Nisa, I went and got the photo album," Ezekiel announces.

"Okay, bring it on, Zeek, I wonder how many of my own pictures are in here. But to answer your question, Ava, the picture you are speaking about was a New Year's Eve party that I was on my way to with your mom and my college homies when I was a fashion student in New York."

"That was a crazy night, we almost got kidnapped!" I add hysterically.

"Times Square was way different back then, compared to how it is now," Nisa says, browsing the photo album.

"Your Auntie Nisa went through a crimps and flipped ponytail phase."

"That's right, until you burnt my hair off!"

The children chatter in disbelief: "No way!" "What!" "Mom wouldn't do that!"

"Yes she did, it was an accident though. Back then she used these Marcelle crimpers, right, and the curling iron stove over-heated the crimper. She spritzed my hair and took a section of my hair right over here by my left ear and put that iron right onto my own hair and held it for like five seconds. She then opens the crimping iron and my hair on this side, was then a half inch long!" Nisa says, laughing as she recalls the incident. "My hair was stuck to those crimpers when she pulled it back! I looked in the mirror like, Jadirah, I'm going to kill you! She's lucky I love her. She broke my hair off and that's how I started my short-cut phase!"

"You sure did, and now people are making custom units off of your signature cut that I, Jadirah, styled for you! That cut is iconic!" I say proudly.

"Is this the haircut, Auntie?" Ava holds up a picture from the photo album.

"Goodness, yes! Look, Tony." She then hands the picture to Tony so that he may see it.

"Oh okay! I see you! Now this is a classic," Tony says, smiling as he views the picture. "How old were you in this pic?"

"I was seventeen and a freshman in college!!" Nisa responds

"So you started college ahead of Mommy?" asks Ava.

"She did, baby, she was so smart she got skipped up a grade. I was a senior in high school when Nisa went to New York for college. Will you set the table? Food is almost ready," I instruct Ava.

"Yes ma'am."

"Now I think that this picture was taken the night that you met Carlos, sis! Look!" Nisa brings me the picture to look at.

"Yes, that was the night you introduced us. Jakka's solo album release party, right?"

"Mmm hmm, you know, so your dad was helping your uncle Jakka develop a clothing line and he was a fine arts student in school with me at the time," Nisa begins as she takes the pictures and places them carefully back into the photo album.

"Jakka used to be in a group called 'The Rugged Brothas' and they did well. I met him when he was in that group on their video shoot that I was styling. He left the group and went solo, and the night that he launched his album, I introduced your mom to your dad. Jakka wore the crown as a hip hop mogul and we were part of his creative team. Your mom styled videos and fashion shows for him. I helped to conceptualize and execute ideas and your father was the lead designer for Jakkawear men's line. I was the lead designer for Jakkawear women's line. That started making us some serious money for some North Philly kids."

"That's right, and now, your Uncle Jakka…" I place the casserole dish with rice and vegetables down upon the dinner table. "…is worth half a billion dollars! Thanks to your Auntie Nisa!" I turn to get the salmon patties and the dinner rolls.

"Whoa, really!" asks Ezekiel.

"Yes really, and now he's doing more with his career. He's in movies, a judge on 'Americas Top Voice,' and this year he's hosting the Static Awards!"

Tony clears his throat. "Jadirah, all of this food looks so good! And you know I'm ready to eat. Where can I wash my hands?" Tony asks.

"Right down the hall to the left; Isaiah, David, all y'all go wash for dinner," I instruct the children so that Nisa and I can chat privately if just for a moment. I look over my shoulder to see if the coast is clear.

"Sis," I whisper. "I noticed that."

"Noticed what?" Nisa replies.

"Don't do that, I noticed Tony's energy and body language while you were talking about Jakka. What's up?"

Nisa rolls her eyes as she stands from the dining table to go and wash her hands. "We'll talk later," she says with a sigh.

After we say a prayer of gratitude, we begin to dine. During dinner, the children make small talk about school and their activities. I am glad we've had an early dinner. I'm hopeful that Carlos will stay out the rest of the day.

"Sis, the Asiatic rice turned out real good!" Nisa says between chews. "It's almost as good as Granny Faye's."

"Oh, now, that's a complement. You know it's my turn to take the supplies out there today," I reply.

"Okay, I ought to ride with you to see Sister Faye. I wanna see the rest of the house, too. The last time I was in town you all were still in the condo."

"You got it!" I reply as I take my empty plate to the kitchen sink.

"Mom, may I have seconds?" Isaiah asks.

"Sure you can, honey. Let me make your dad a plate and set it aside first though. Okay?"

"Yes ma'am."

"You have always been a sweetheart, Jay," Nisa says after overhearing the exchange between my son and I. While placing her plate in the sink, Nisa asks if I am feeling alright. I nod yes and tell her to help me clean the countertop. I instruct Ava to put away any leftovers so that I may give Nisa and Tony a tour of our home.

"So you all have seen the foyer, the kitchen, the dining area, powder room and living room. So the first thing we'll do is start up the stairs."

We walk up the stairs and start with the boys room. "So this is the second largest bedroom. This is David, Zeek, and 'Saiah's room. I guess it's obvious with the bunk beds and posters and all."

Nisa strolls on into the room and takes a look around. She looks out the window and into their closet in silence. We step back out into the hallway to continue the tour.

"This is the restroom, and that's Ava's room right here to the left," I continue. Nisa places her hands in her pockets and walks into Ava's room.

"This is a nice layout, Jadirah, how long had it been on the market?" Tony asks.

"About ten months, I think. Carlos picked this place out driving down the street," I reply. I notice Nisa opening Ava's closet. "Well, what are your thoughts, inspector? Does everything meet up to your approval?" I say jokingly.

"You want to know what I'm thinking? I'm thinking my baby girl needs some more dresses if she's out here making straight A's," she says, walking out of the bedroom.

"Okay, so now this is the master suite, correct?" Nisa says, pointing to mine and Carlos' bedroom.

"Yep, straight ahead." We walk in. "This is the ensuite to the right and that is the closet right there. Sorry about all this messy laundry in here."

"No, it's cool. Where are your shoes?" Nisa asks.

"On my side of the bed by that grey dresser."

Nisa walks over to take a look. Her eyes dance around the bedroom, sizing everything up. She's always been observant. I begin to wonder. "This is the closet right here?" Nisa says as she walks into the closet.

"Yep!" I reply.

Nisa walks in and starts going through our closet. She looks at Carlos' Air Jordan collection with a frown on her face. "Where are your clothes, sis?"

"This black patch here, you know I get color on everything so, all black like the omen," I joke. Clearly, she's not amused.

Nisa then asks in her serious tone of voice as her eyes dance throughout Carlos' wardrobe. "Sis, where do you keep all those shoes, handbags, and clothes that I sent you?" Nisa asks.

"I keep those items hidden, I would have a fit if some bleach or jelly ended up on any $500 blouse. Girl, that bag that you sent me was $6,000 on their website!" I explain to Nisa.

"Yeah, well I got it for free once the merger went through," she says, walking out from our quaint closet. Her eyebrows are raised and her lips firmly pressed together.

Is she not pleased with our home? Why do I feel like she is unimpressed? As we walk back down the stairs, I decide to eschew a conversation about her sudden attitude. As we start back toward the kitchen area, where the children are, we hear keys rattling against the front door. It's Carlos, and by the looks of the second shadow behind his, Ronnie is with him.

They enter the foyer and Tony, Nisa and I are looking right at them both. "I knew it!" Carlos begins with a wide grin, snatching off his glasses and placing them on the side table.

"Yo! Nisa Hyatt right in front of me. Yo, I'm buggin right now!" Ronnie adds.

"Hey guys!" Nisa greets them with a polite smile.

"I saw that Bentley out front and I knew you were in here! Where's my hug at, sis!" Carlos says, reaching for a hug.

I then instruct Ronnie to place his cellphone in the wicker basket, on the table next to the front door if he wants to stay awhile. These are the rules when a high-profile guest like Nisa Hyatt comes to visit our home. As I observe Ronnie's body language and energy, it becomes clear that he may be a little star-struck from the way that he's gazing at Nisa while she and Carlos exchange pleasantries.

"Carlos, I want to introduce you to Anthony Grant. This is my business partner. Anthony, this is Carlos," Nisa says.

"What's up, brother, good to meet you!" Tony says, extending his hand to Carlos for a handshake.

"Good to meet you also," Carlos says, shaking hands with Tony. "Y'all, this is *my* business partner and friend, Ronald, we all just call him Ronnie."

Ronnie hugs Nisa like he's known her for years. Carlos panics for a moment and starts to pull Ronnie off of Nisa because he's gotten a little too excited. Nisa makes eye contact with Carlos and mouths silently, "It's alright, I'm cool." Carlos looks at me and shakes his head at Ronnie's fanboy behavior. I roll my eyes and shake my head at Carlos.

"Whoa, Nisa Hyatt! I've always wanted to meet you and Carlos always said to the fellas on the basketball squad that he knew you and Jakka and that you all were the kids' godparents!" Ronnie states.

Nisa slowly pulls Ronnie off of her and places both of her hands upon his for a handshake as if she's teaching him how to show a little decorum when meeting celebrities. "Well," she begins with a chuckle, "Carlos is not lying. It's a pleasure to meet you, Ronnie," Nisa says in a professional manner.

"Carlos, I told Anthony about your business plans. I also told him about the app that you and Ronnie are developing," I announce.

"Yeah, Ronnie and I had planned to work on it today, as a matter of fact! Let me go and get my laptop out of the office. Jadirah, baby, could you come help me out?" Carlos says excitedly.

"Sure, I'll be right there. Y'all want to just go to the kitchen table and make yourselves comfortable. Okay? We'll be right back," I instruct as I head up the stairs to the bedroom. I get into the bedroom and hear the shower running. Carlos comes out of the ensuite, pulling off his sweatshirt. I close the bedroom door.

"Why didn't you tell me that Nisa was coming over here today?!?" Carlos says frantically, pulling his socks off.

"You know why. You remember what happened last time!" I say firmly.

"Well, anyway, is Jakka coming too? I really need to talk to him. He hasn't responded to any of my emails or DMs!"

"Jakka is not coming."

"Okay, well I can't meet, smelling like the gym. I'm gonna take a quick shower and I'll be right down."

"Okay, I'll let everyone know," I say, heading toward the bedroom door to exit.

I hesitate just a moment before I go back into the kitchen. I hope that I don't regret setting this meeting up between Tony and Carlos. I didn't expect for Ronnie's silly ass to be over here today. I hope that they don't embarrass themselves in front of *the* Anthony Grant, a successful businessman, venture capitalist and motivational speaker.

The children are in the family room; I decide to speak to them first. "Hey y'all, when your father comes downstairs I want you all to go into my room to watch TV, ok?"

"Could we get our phones back? Please, Mom, we won't do anything!" Ezekiel asks.

"Sure honey, but please, *please* don't break any rules. Ok?"

"Yes ma'am" they respond.

I start toward the kitchen and I hear Tony, Ronnie, and Nisa making small talk. "So, Anthony, where did you go to school, man?" Ronnie begins.

"I'm straight up proud Bison, my brotha!" Tony says lightheartedly.

"Ok, okay, D.C.? H.U.? Good for you."

"I love D.C., I love the culture, I love the GoGo!" I add.

"I would not have been focused if I would have went to school in D.C., I would've been kickin' it everyday, you know what I'm saying," Ronnie says, laughing.

"You would've done just fine, bro! The professors there are built differently. They become like your aunts and uncles. It's really about making the most of it," Tony states.

"Well, what worked for you?" Ronnie asks, sipping his drink.

"Willpower, restraint and discipline. Straight like that," Tony says, nodding.

I take my seat at the table next to Nisa. "Carlos wanted to hop in the shower real quick, y'all, he'll be right down," I tell them.

"No worries, we're just chillin," Nisa says with a smile as she nudges me.

We continue on with small talk of entertainment and sports when suddenly, Carlos comes down the stairs reading loudly: "Nisa Hyatt is indeed a mega mogul. Shattering the expectations of many with her business acumen and her daring vision to vanquish industries beyond the limitations of the fashion and entertainment world. An international business woman with a professional disposition such as Michelle O. A hustler's mentality similar to Damon Dash and reality show persona similar to the fictional Diva herself, Miranda Priestly. Understanding this powerhouse means to understand what drive is, personified." Carlos ends the magazine quote from Nisa's interview with Radical Fashion Magazine. He is standing at the kitchen table and flops the magazine down upon the table. "How does that make you feel, sis?" Carlos asks Nisa.

"What, the magazine article? It's cool, it's accurate," Nisa says confidently, sipping her coffee. "Anyway, the app. What's up with your business plan? We don't have a lot of time," Nisa says, switching to business mode.

"Okay, well, our app is different from the others," Carlos says, opening his laptop. "What it is, is a social network for individuals looking for inspiration and different ideas, hobbies, styles for men or women…"

Ronnie then interrupts: "And what it also does is helps people figure out a look for or a theme for say maybe a retirement party or a New Year's Eve party, it would give you pictures or images of ideas to help you to create a vision for what it is that you are trying to plan for," he adds.

Carlos slides the laptop over to Tony and Tony shoots Nisa a look of discontent. "See, here are some mock images of how the setup would be and the user would be able to scroll through the images, tap on the ones that they are interested in using for inspiration, and save them," Carlos says.

"Yeah and the concept is like a personal magazine, except it's at your fingertips on your smartphone or iPad!" Ronnie adds excitedly.

"Okay, guys, I understand," Tony says, looking at the screen. He then rubs the side of his face as if he's trying to find words. "Can I say something, fellas?" he asks.

"Sure, anything you want!" Carlos says, moving the laptop back in front of himself.

"Do you have a name for this app?"

"No, not yet, we have a few ideas for the name."

"Ok, I'm not a beat-around-the-bush kind of guy so I'm just going to come right out and say it… This app that you all are working on sounds like Pinterest," Tony says in a matter-of-fact manner.

Ronnie and Carlos are silent.

"Do you all know what Pinterest is?" Tony asks arrogantly.

"Of course we know what Pinterest is. This app will be nothing like that," Carlos says defensively.

"I mean no offense, my brother, but if you want this idea to work, it's going to have to be a breath of fresh air. The app market is saturated as it is. What you all will need to do is fine tune this concept and make it stand out, that's all I'm saying."

Nisa stands up at the awkward silence of Ronnie and Carlos. "I'm gonna grab another glass of juice," Nisa announces as she raises her eyebrows.

I nervously begin to make more small talk. Carlos shuts down his laptop as if he is defeated by Tony's critique. I observe Ronnie's vibe and he seems fine.

"So Anthony, ahh… what kind of business are *you* in?" Carlos asks, sizing Tony up.

"I'm a venture capitalist and an entrepreneur," Tony answers.

"Ok, so how many businesses do you have?" Ronnie asks.

"Approximately nine, and two nonprofits," Tony answers.

"We also have 43 investments," Nisa adds.

"Oh, you and Jakka?" Carlos adds.

"Tony and I," Nisa answers quickly. "Jakka has his own business partner, he has this whole machine working 24/7 for ventures."

"Don't I know it, I've been trying to get ahold of him. I know he hasn't gone Hollywood on me! We made a lot of money together. I think he would understand my business plans if I could just talk with him. That's my guy and we go way back," Carlos says in a prideful way.

"I'll see what I can do, I mean… he is super busy," Nisa says, taking her seat.

"I'm family though, I was there at the beginning." Carlos notices Tony's unfamiliar wrist watch. "Where did you find this watch at, Tony? At the Juneteenth festival or something?" Carlos asks.

Ronnie chuckles, "From one of the vendor tables, bro."

Nisa and I look at one another. Carlos' ego is running wild and he is triggered to save face. Directing the attention away from his feeling of rejection, he turns to the outsider to dump on.

"Actually, this is a Kuji watch. KUJI wrist watch, short for Kujichagulia, or self-determination. My frat brother just started his watch business and I'm always down to support black-owned business. As a matter of fact, I'm thinking of investing maybe about fifty racks or so," Tony says, making eye contact with Carlos.

"Well, that's nice, black business. More power to him! I'm going to stick with my Rolex, though," Carlos says recklessly, trying to insult Tony.

Tony brushes if off. He understands what's happening.

"You know what, Jadirah, will you call the kids down here? I want to give them something," Nisa says.

"What you trying to give my babies?" Carlos asks.

"Some cash to get dessert! We didn't have dessert after dinner. Can Isaiah drive? You know, maybe they should walk, it's a nice day," Nisa says, going through her purse.

I call the children downstairs. I then instruct them to walk up to the local store for pound-cake. They put on their shoes and their jackets and start on the task at hand. The adults need to talk and we need time. The children leave and we all settle down a bit.

"I don't know, Nisa, I thought we were all family. Jakka has been avoiding me and I need to talk to him, we need to get the clothing line back going on! I've got fresh new designs that I've been working on!" Carlos says.

"Carlos, why do you think I'm here?" Nisa says, folding her arms.

Carlos is silent for a moment. He knows why she is here. Even Ronnie knows why Nisa is here! She's here out of concern for me and the children and how we are coming along from all of the public drama of the repossession.

"Of course I know why you're here! You are here to visit with your godchildren and you miss home, Philly is home!"

Nisa looks at him and tilts her head to the side. "I am here to address the elephant in the room head on," Nisa says.

"Uhh, maybe I better get going," Ronnie interrupts.

"No, you can stay. It's my house, you can stay, bro," Carlos says.

"My sis was publicly humiliated, Carlos…"

Carlos interrupts Nisa as he smacks his teeth and says, "Is that what we're doing today? Beating a dead horse?"

"…No, I wish to understand your part in it. You have a really good job and I went through this before. If you stick to a budget, you have more than enough to afford your lifestyle."

"Do *you* stick to a budget? Tony, do you?" Carlos asks.

"As a matter of fact, I do. I live off of $29,000 a year," Tony replies.

"Well, you better than me! I can't do that, I got four kids. Nisa, you and Jakka got two kids, do y'all stick to a budget with all the money y'all got?" Carlos says angrily.

"Yes, we do! Let me tell you something, celebrities get free stuff all of the time. Those dresses you see me wear on those red carpets are gifts from the designers. It's people who always *spending* their money who are always broke. Bro, we are too damn old to be mismanaging money, y'all got four kids, my godkids. You owe it to them to stop putting yourself first, bro."

"Putting myself first!?"

"Yes! You know you put yourself first. Jadirah is still driving that same BMW from back in the day! You have a new Range Rover that you can't afford! I got a tour of the house and I couldn't believe my eyes at your shoe collection! I saw a $4,000 Versace coat! Jakka has one just like it! You have no business having your wife out here, ass-out like that. I nearly died when I saw that video! Jadirah is too much of a sweetheart and I'm here as a sister-friend to you both. The mismanagement of funds needs to stop immediately. It gets harder the older you get…"

Suddenly Tony's cellphone vibrates on the table and interrupts Nisa. She stands at attention and looks at the face of his phone. "It's Joshua," she sings excitedly with her eyebrows raised. "Can he take this call, you guys? We have been waiting on this call all day!"

"Sure, go right ahead, Tony!" I answer. Carlos nods with interest in what this call might be about.

"Joshua! How's it goin?" Tony answers. Nisa looking to read Tony's facial expressions for good news. "I did get the email and I reviewed the report and there are a few concerns that we should discuss regarding the rate."

You could hear a pin drop. Even Ronnie was silent to try to figure out the conversation taking place.

"Yeah, that's not what we discussed," Tony says firmly on the call. Nisa leans in to whisper some business to him. He glances at her and nods. "Yeah mmm hmm… Ok. Look, Joshua, seventeen percent—or there is nothing else to speak about." Nisa looks at the table in a gaze and slowly nods. "Okay, I'll look for that email shortly, Josh. Thanks, buddy," Tony ends the call and whispers some words to Nisa.

"Okay," Nisa replies quietly to Tony.

"Y'all doing some business? Closing a deal or something, Nisa?" Carlos asks curiously.

Nisa simply smiles at him. "Now you know I can't talk about that. Anyway, where was I… Oh yes, budgeting. Not keeping to a budget gets harder as you get older because of the children. They are going to start college soon and thank God we got the college account set up for them!"

I quickly hop up from the table and go into the kitchen. I know that Nisa is going to lose it when she finds out that Carlos has spent all of the children's college money that she and Jakka setup for them.

She notices my energy right away. "Jadirah, what's up?" Nisa asks. I turn to look at her and I shake my head quickly. "Carlos, what is up, what is the vibe I just caught?"

Carlos scratches his head and reluctantly begins. "I had to use the money for some investments," he replies.

"How much?" Nisa says as the anger grows within her.

"Why do you even care, you're rich!"

"Carlos, how much of the money was used?"

"All of it!"

Nisa's eyes widen as she exhales in disbelief. "What?!? You wasted $100,000!?! Do you not give a *fuck* about your own children, either!?!"

"I took the money and invested in a food truck business, it's on hold right now but it's coming along. Don't rush to judgment, Nisa, damn!"

"Carlos, you are a smart man, but not very wise. You are someone who makes excuses and poor business choices. You can always be found procrastinating and inevitably your choice will be made for you by circumstance. I cannot believe you took the kids' money. Why would you do that?"

"My kids are smart enough to get scholarships, they are going to be fine. But what we are not going to do is gang up on Carlos! No! We will see a return on that investment before you know it!"

"Face it, Carlos, you don't care about your wife or your kids. Period!" Nisa says angrily.

Carlos is silent for a moment. Clearly annoyed and offended, he takes a deep breath. "You of all people are judging me? Carlos, Carlos, Carlos, huh. Does Tony over here know the real you? Does he know that you went to jail for trying to kill someone? Is your business partner aware of who your mother was and what she used to do for a little bit of dope? Hey, guess what, Tony? Do you know how I met Nisa at school? She was my weed dealer! She sold coke, did credit card fraud, but now… You want to sit here and judge me like you better than everybody else, trying to emasculate me in front of my wife and Ronnie. I don't even know Anthony but you just want to go in on me. Y'all come into my house all bougie and stuck up… Oh, how is your brother, Nisa? Is he still at Riker's Island? Yeah, Tony, now he was one murdering, drug-dealing muthafucka! Isn't that right, Nisa?" Carlos says with a smirk.

"Yo, that was unnecessary, bro. Nisa, we'd better get going," Tony says, standing up from the dining chair.

"No," Nisa says, gazing at Carlos. Her face is tight and her eyes widened. "I am not ready to go," she says calmly.

I haven't seen this look in her eyes since we were girls. She's clearly triggered and I'm afraid that things will get ugly. I mean, I have seen her fist fight grown men before.

"Nisa, Nisa…?" I ask.

"Yeah, I'm good," she replies. "My past isn't pretty, so what I'm from nothing. I don't know who I would have been if Pops and Mama Diane wouldn't have taken me in, and when I left home for New York I learned to support myself! I survived! I did what I felt was necessary for self-preservation. I was determined to do the impossible…"

Carlos interrupts. "See, that's what I'm trying to do! But you from the gutter too, is all I'm saying!"

"…Negro, please," Nisa calmly shakes her head with her eyes closed. "You can't use what I've already accepted about myself against me! I'm well aware of my flaws. Nice try, though! You wanna get real, bro? We can get real but peep this… I'm nowhere near as gentle as Jadirah. See, I could care less about your ego or the fact that you are broken and grew up in a crack house. Name me one nigga from the hood who didn't struggle. The strong survive, the lame ones don't make it…"

There's a sudden knock at the front door. I panic. Who could it be? We are not expecting anyone. "Carlos, are you expecting someone?" I ask.

"No, I'm not," Carlos responds.

"Nisa, run up to my room and hide!" I instruct.

Nisa runs upstairs and shuts the bedroom door. Carlos looks out the side window, expecting it to be nosy neighbors because of the Bentley parked outside. "Oh shit," Carlos exclaims.

"Who is it?" Ronnie asks.

"It's my mom and Lil Bit," Carlos answers. "I'm going to let them in."

I sigh. "Alright, here we go," I say aloud.

The two women enter the foyer and they reek of alcohol and cheap perfume. Lil Bit is as ghetto as they come. Her make-up is horrible. Purple lipstick and drawn on eyebrows reminiscent of Homie the Clown! She smacks her chewing gum loudly and I'm already anxious for them to leave.

"Hey, world's greatest son!" Carlos' mother, Bev, says. "Oh, how you doing, Jadirah, does your face feel better, honey?"

"How are you, Ms. Bev? Hey, Lil Bit," I say to them.

"Hey baby," Lil Bit says.

"What is up, Mom, is something wrong?" Carlos asks her.

"Well, you wasn't pickin up your phone and I was… well!" She looks at Tony and loses her train of thought. "Who is this tall drank of water over here! How you been doin?"

"Hello ladies," Tony says.

"Mom, Lil Bit, this is Anthony Grant, we were having a business meeting with him," Carlos adds.

"Oh, so is that your ride out front, handsome?" Lil Bit says in her husky smoker's voice.

"Ah, yes ma'am, it is," Tony says reluctantly.

They look at him as if he is an all-you-can-eat buffet. He's clearly uncomfortable and everyone notices.

"So, Mom! What can I do for you?" Carlos says, frustrated.

"Can I talk to you in the kitchen? Just real quick, I wasn't trying to interrupt your lil meeting," Bev asks.

"Okay, come on."

As Ms. Bev and Carlos head toward the kitchen, Ronnie starts to joke around with Lil Bit. I wonder if I should grab my phone to check on the children. I know that they are on their way back. I hear the change pot in the kitchen. Ms. Bev came out here for some money. Lil Bit is her driver and they are probably trying to get high tonight.

"Okay, we'll catch y'all later! Bye, little Jadirah," Ms. Bev says as she pets the top of my head like a puppy. I let it slide, I want them gone. Carlos lets them out of the door and we all wait patiently for them to pull off. They ride away and I go to inform Nisa.

I knock on the door. "Hey sis, they're gone," I say.

"Okay, alright," she says on the phone.

"Who is that on the line?" I ask.

"Jakka, he wants to holler at you real quick." She hands me the phone.

We exchange greetings and he asks about the children. We make small talk for a moment. I know that who he really wants to speak to… is Carlos. Jakka has been known for giving verbal lashings to men who don't handle their business.

"Are you feeling ok, sis? Nisa just broke the news to me," Jakka asks.

"Yes, I'm fine, I'm tough, I'll be alright," I answer.

"If you need anything, anything at all—chemo, access to a specialist, anything at all…" he continues.

"I know, I love you brother," I reply.

"I love you too, sis, lemme speak to Carlos real quick," Jakka orders.

"Okay."

Nisa snatches the phone. "Like I was saying, let me know, okay?" Nisa says, charging out of the room headed toward the stairs. I'm right behind her. "Here, Carlos, Jakka wants to speak to you," Nisa says, handing him the phone.

Carlos' face lights up with optimism and then concern sets on his face; maybe he thinks he's in trouble for speaking to

Nisa recklessly earlier. "Hey Nisa, I apologize for things getting heated earlier, you know that's how family do sometimes!" Carlos says loud enough for Jakka to hear on the other end of the line.

"Yeah, yeah, whatever! Fuck it!" Nisa says nonchalantly, grabbing her coat and making quiet small talk with Tony.

"Yo Jakka! Peace, brethren, how you been? I had been trying to get ahold of you but..." Carlos voice trails off. Apparently Jakka has a few things to get off of his chest because Carlos is as quiet as a church mouse. "...Ok, you got it. Good to hear from you, Jakka. Peace," Carlos concludes as he hands Nisa's phone back to her.

The children arrive with the dessert items. I greet them and tell them to set everything up. I approach Nisa in the quiet corner of the living room to see what's going on and I hear her talking.

"Okay but that's it, two more appearances and we're good," Nisa says.

"Yes, you have my word. We sure have come a long way from where we started, Nisa. I'm proud of you," Jakka says.

Nisa pauses, "Yeah, me too. You... take care, okay?" She ends the call.

"What was that, sis? Is everything alright?" I ask.

"I want to tell you later, this isn't the time and place," Nisa says, looking over my shoulder. "Tony, I've decided to go with Jadirah to Grandma Faye's house."

"Are you sure?" Tony says reluctantly, with tenderness in his voice.

"Yeah, I need to clear my head. Will you call Tabitha when you get back to the hotel and tell her that we are going to move forward with that real estate project?"

"I certainly will, are you all leaving now?"

"Yes," we both reply simultaneously.

"Okay, then, I am too," Tony says with a smile.

Nisa and Tony exchange evening cordials with Carlos, Ronnie, and all of the children as I instruct Isaiah and Ezekiel to load the bulk items into my truck for their great-grandmother. In this moment, I feel grateful that my friend is here to help me make room for my abundance. Her example of strength and the fact that she survived everything, every challenge thrown at her, is inspiring.

I have to admit that I am now comfortable with the idea of facing this cancer. I plan to survive it.

EIGHT

Umi Says

W e're almost there, Nisa! It's not as far as you think," I say.

"I forgot about this side of Pennsylvania out here in the boondocks! I feel like Michael Myers or Jason is gonna come out of those trees and get us!" Nisa adds, laughing.

"Girl, you so silly! I love it out here, it's so peaceful. I see why Grandma is still out here living her very best life."

"Yeah, I guess you're right… I need this right now, the city is all hustle and bustle. You know that therapist that the network made me go to told me to go out into the country and rest my mind. To… seek solitude. Thanks for letting me drive today."

We are silent for a few moments.

"You know you was wrong for pushing that girl, I would have sent your ass to therapy too!" I say with a smirk.

"She shouldn't have been running her mouth! You saw that episode, right? She called me Ghetto Trash on national

TV! Now, you know me, you've known me my whole life, and I've never tolerated disrespect."

"Is the therapy helping you manage your temper?"

"Yeah, it's helping. You see how I kept it together with Carlos' ignorant ass back at your house. And… it's helped me manage the pressure, Jakka and his baby mammas. You know, we haven't been intimate in two years."

"He still only has the extra two kids right?"

"Yep."

"Does Junior and little Jadirah know about their… extra siblings?"

"Not that I know of, they've never questioned me about it."

"Jakka knows about you and Tony?"

"What do you mean?"

"It is a little obvious, sis, I seen how he looks at you."

"Girl, what? How does he look at me?"

"How Sticks looks at Sparkle!" I say, laughing.

"I got too much going on, he deserves a woman with less baggage."

"I can tell he loves you."

Nisa smacks her teeth and shakes her head. She's sensitive about sharing things about her and Jakka's dysfunctional relationship. It's been all over social media and in the blogs. Jakka's last big lawsuit was settled out of court; "The Threesome Gone Wrong" was on the headlines from the fashion show in Paris. One of the two women accused him of battery and that Jakka broke her front teeth out. I never questioned Nisa about it because… it's embarrassing.

"We've arrived!" Nisa says cheerfully, pulling into my grandmother's driveway.

"Okay, we can't stay long if it's dark out, she'll make us spend the night!" I say sternly.

"Are you serious?" Nisa says, shutting the car off.

My grandmother's house is a ranch-style brick home on five acres of land. She does have an impressive garden that she raises every year during springtime. No animals. She's comfortable, she hates the city. I love her. Every time I come out here for a visit, it's a new experience.

I look over and notice Nisa grabbing the large bag of brown rice that we've brought out of the trunk of my car with ease. She's still got that helpful heart after all these years. Even with all of her wealth, success and status. She's marching bulk items up to grandma's door with $3,000 boots on!

As we approach the door, Grandma Faye comes out onto the porch to greet us. "Alright now, you made it, baby!" she says cheerfully. "Peace, peace, peace, now get on in here and put all that stuff down, ladies, and give me a good hug!"

We oblige, looking forward to her warm hugs and kisses. She has always hugged tight, with a rocking motion from side to side accompanied with grateful laughter and approximately three kisses on the cheek. I usually chuckle along with her, but today, I smile and simply close my eyes.

"And here is my other grandbaby, Nisa!" she says, reaching for her hug. Nisa willfully embraces grandmother. "Look at you, all glamorous, marching up my driveway. I read about you in the magazine that my Raheem brought up here," she says, releasing the hug and looking into Nisa's face. "The article says that you are rich and successful. You've made something out of yourself and that's good! I didn't expect to see you today..." she pauses, "I want to know that your soul and spirit is rich and successful, alright!"

"Yes ma'am" we both reply.

"Okay, okay, come on in and take your shoes off," she instructs.

Grandma Faye's house smells like her famous navy bean soup. Green bell peppers and yellow onions sautéed to perfection and her wheat muffins. It's always impeccably clean and she has to have about one thousand books. In our family, we do what she tells us, she has survived so much. She is our sensei, a saint and a teacher in our eyes. She carries herself like a relic of a lost ancient civilization. She fosters culture, pride and knowledge of self. I can only dream of reaching her level of perfect enlightenment. When we ask her what she is or how do you identify yourself, she says, "I am an *original* woman." When asked about her religious affiliations, she'll always reply, "I am Muslim, I am an organic Christian, I am a Hebrew, I am a Child of God." Which means, *I am something only a few can understand.*

"You all need to come on in the kitchen! Let me fix you a bowl of soup. I know that I've probably told you this, but me and the sisters had the opportunity to fix dinner for The Greatest Boxer of All Times! I did the bean soup and he cleaned the bowl!" she says pridefully. "I still can't believe he is gone, may God be pleased with him."

"Grandma, we just ate dinner at Jadirah's house!" Nisa announces.

"Oh, well, I don't want you to over eat, I better give y'all a very small portion," she says as she prepares small bowls of bean soup.

Nisa gives me a look that says, "Oh lord, my waist line!"

I smile and wink as Grandmother sets the tiny bowls down on the kitchen table. "Now come on and sit and eat! Don't let it get cold," she demands.

We sit and eat within two minutes. Grandma does not believe in over eating at all!

"Now Jadirah, I spoke with your mama last week and she said you and Carlos are having problems?"

"Yes, ma'am, they just don't make'em like they used to! I grew up watching Dad take good care of Mom."

"That's cause I raised your dad the right way!"

"I just want to be loved properly, that old school love that you and Granddaddy had."

Grandma sighs. "Baby, look here, your grandpa wasn't shit," she says, laughing.

Nisa nearly chokes on her soup and then sips her water. Shocked, I ask Grandma why she would say such a thing.

"Sweetheart, y'all are old enough to get the truth about things; when y'all were little, it wasn't for children to know about grown-up business. Your grandfather and I were married at sixteen years old. I had four children by the time I was twenty-one. I left him down there in Tennessee to go live with my sister Roberta in Harlem! I converted to Islam in the early '60s and those brothers stood tall and were examples for your dad and uncles. I had four little black boys to raise in Harlem of all places. Your grandfather had five more kids out of wedlock from cheating. I moved away because I was humiliated in that small little county."

Nisa and I are silent.

"Men aren't very strong, not strong like us," she stands and clears our empty bowls from the table. "Let's go outside, I want to show you my plants!" she orders.

She goes into her room to grab Nisa a spare pair of gardening boots. She gets around exceptionally well to be in her early eighties. She always says it's because she eats one meal a day and she walks for one hour straight, daily.

She takes us around the backyard to show us where she'll be planting her vegetables and herb garden. It's always so peaceful and she's always got some good jazz or soul music going. She used to always teach us about dance therapy and she always said that the right music will always defeat depression. Definitely something she picked up when she lived in Africa for three years.

As we venture back into the house, I let her know that we'd better get going soon.

"Before you all go, I need to make sure you all are covered, baby. Get two chairs and put them in the living room, so that I may speak life and pray over you," she says in a caring tone.

We do as she asks. I feel a little anxious because I always cry when Grandma prays. "I haven't done this in years, sis," Nisa says, moving her chair.

We place our chairs beside each other and Grandma puts on Yusef Lateef, a jazz musician that she's always loved. "He brings a sacred energy through music," Grandma says as the record begins. Dressed in coveralls, a colorful head wrap covering her silver French braids, and holding a Chowrie with dress fabric sewn on the top that belonged to Great Grandmother. "It is used to tap life and spirit from the ancestors," says my grandmother.

This is something that she picked up from the tribe she lived with in Africa. Grandma begins the prayer. We close our eyes to get in tune. "I come before The Most High today to ask for favor and victory!" she begins with a booming voice. "Oh Father, make us free from want of what is beside thee. I speak words and words have power! I speak onto my grandchildren Nisa and Jadirah. Please! Bless them with:

"Wisdom! Abundance! Prosperity! Freedom! Success! Love! Patience! Kindness! Fearlessness! Fearlessness! Fearlessness!" She prays while tapping the African Chowrie, draped with the fabric of my great-grandmother, gently against my left shoulder and Nisa's right shoulder. I begin to well up with tears. I feel the presence of sacred holy energy. I suddenly hear Nisa softly weeping. She feels God's divine presence, too.

"Please remove, Father: Self-Doubt! Anger! Hurt! Pain! Shame! Revenge! Negative thought! Confusion! Please, Father! Remove anybody that brings them down! Protect their hearts! Let them tap into their divine self and listen to you for guidance, Father!"

By this point Nisa begins weeping. No control. Sobbing. She's let go. Grandma Faye has clearly struck a spiritual nerve. Nisa never cries! The only time I've seen her cry was at her father's funeral.

Grandmother continues: "For they are your children, open their hearts. Amen."

I open my teary eyes to look at Nisa, and my grandmother embraces her as she sits and begins to weep with a howl that I've never seen before. She even stomps her foot a few times while weeping. I quickly hop up to grab tissue paper.

Grandma begins to speak softly to her while they embrace. "Alright baby, release it, that's right, let it go. It's going to be alright."

I hand Grandma some tissue paper and keep a little to clean my tears from my face. Nisa had to be crying for five minutes straight. I feel sad, but I'm also glad that she is around the safety of loved ones to release all of that built-up pain and anger that she's held in for years.

Grandmother rubs Nisa's back gently as she releases from the embrace and instructs her to get around family and loved ones more often, and to nurture her relationship with the Most High, so that she won't become spiritually empty. Nisa, wiping her tears, simply nods.

"Grandmother, we thank you for this, we really needed it," I say.

"I know, that's why I requested you for this week," she says, smiling. "Tell Fatimah it's her turn next Saturday!"

"It's still a little light left, we had better get going, Nisa."

Nisa goes to put on her jacket and shoes. We say our goodbyes to the best grandmother in the world. What a beautiful visit, so much meaning! We are so blessed. I have to profess my grandmother's essence is something that I aspire to develop.

NINE

Scheming

Nisa and I are silent on our drive back to Philly. Reflecting. The frequency fused to our spirits.

"You know, Grandma Faye is deep!" Nisa says while reclining the passenger seat. "She's like powerful or something, I know that her prayers are going to be heard."

"I know right, she prays hard. Hey, sis, let me know when you get a signal out here. I'm expecting a call from Fatimah," I state.

"What does she want?"

"She wants to see if I'm going to Daddy's gig tonight."

"Pops got a gig tonight? I wanna go!"

"Are you serious? Tony is gonna be looking for you at the hotel."

"Don't worry about that, I got a plan!"

"Are you cooking up a scheme? Whatchu got up your sleeve, girl?"

Nisa says nothing, she gives a sly grin and raises her eyebrows twice. We get closer to the city and I'm able to call my sister to see if she still wants to go out. She does—she's a new mom and needs a break. Nisa sees an opportunity to have a girl's night.

"If we are all hangin' out, you are gonna need a disguise! I'm not trying to get mobbed again, look, see up there. See that billboard!" I say to Nisa while at a stoplight. It's a picture of Nisa and three other judges from the panel of her reality show.

"Okay well, what you got in this bag back here?" Nisa reaches in the back of the car.

"That's just my gym stuff."

Nisa digs around in the bag and discovers a silk scarf. "Okay, I can wear this, it smells clean, ain't no gel on it!"

"I think you sent me that scarf."

Nisa then ties the scarf around and ties it under her chin, like a church lady. "Look at this scarf…" she says, looking in the passenger side mirror. "… I look like Whitney on the Body Guard movie!" she says, laughing. "*And I I I E E E E E E I I will always love you oooh oooh I I*," she sings terribly.

"Oh gosh, that's awful. We need to get you some shoes. Look back there for those slides."

"Slides! I don't wear slides!"

"That's right, that's the whole point! Goodness gracious, Nisa!"

"Look at these slides, you work in these? Looks like you stole these from an old white lady who lived in Vermont her whole life!"

I sigh, "Just try the damn shoes on!"

We finally arrive at Fatimah's house and Nisa climbs into the back seat of the car to surprise her. I call to let her know that we are in front of her house. She comes down and I unlock the doors so she can hop right in.

"Hey Sis, what's up?" I say.

"Hey Sis, nothin," she responds.

"Boo!" Nisa grabs Fatimah's shoulders from behind her.

"Nisa!! Ahhh," Fatimah screams with delight. "What are you doing in town?"

"I had to come check on Jadirah and the kids," Nisa responds.

"I know right, that whole situation was some bullshit! Fuck Carlos for that shit."

"If only he knew how to be consistent and set his priorities straight, he would have the potential…" I say as Nisa interrupts.

"Yes, he has potential. Always has but shit! Potential won't pay the bills. If you don't have any confidence or wisdom about what you are doing, no plan… sheesh! Your only plan is to latch onto someone's coat-tail is not a plan to success. He is not a boss type, sis. I'm sorry!" Nisa adds.

"That's right, sis, no disrespect but it ain't no room for negotiations when it comes to respect, love is not a reason to tolerate disrespect. As a matter of fact, I think he don't respect you *because* you love him!" Fatimah says.

"Oh sis, that's deep," Nisa says excitedly. "He don't respect you 'cause he is disgusted at you loving him! Damn!"

"Anyway, enough about me! What are y'all trying to get into?" I ask them.

"Well, Dad doesn't start playing for another hour or so," Fatimah says.

"Let's go to our old cheesesteak spot!" Nisa says.

"Alright, let's do it!" I say.

We begin riding through the old stomping grounds of Philadelphia, having fun, making jokes, catching up and enjoying one another. We pick Nisa's cheesesteak order up and she splits it with Fatimah. I am content with my fries and drink. "Fatimah, Grandma Faye will be expecting you next Saturday," Nisa says, eating her fries in the back seat.

"Okay, got you," Fatimah says, sipping her soft drink.

"I feel like she healed me or something. I feel lighter."

"How do you mean?" I ask, stopping at a red light.

"Healed from like, disappointments, adolescent trauma, childhood pains. I feel like she used her knowledge of life to help me heal my wounds," Nisa adds.

"I understand what you mean, Grandma is a gem. I love her so much."

"Y'all are so blessed, don't take it for granted… Y'all are so lucky."

"No, sis, *we* are so lucky!" I say as I turn to look at her.

"That's right, girl! We! Are lucky, we are blessed, you are our sister! And we are proud of you! Grandma Faye is your granny too! So let's get it on and live it up and get girls night on and poppin!" Fatimah says hysterically.

We all crack up laughing and head over to Smitty's, where Dad's band is playing tonight. When we pull up, we can hear the live music sounding good from the parking lot. Nisa looks hilarious in her shades with her disguise.

I look at my crew and the energy is right and the closeness feels like old times.

When we stop at the door, Dad's real good friend Charlie is at the door and he lets us in with no cover charge. Smitty's club is a quaint, moody-lit space with round tables and a dance floor. The bar area is always packed; they sell wings, fries and fish dinners.

Dad is on stage performing as we look for a place to sit. The band sounds good and the vibe is cool. The song that they are performing is ending and the crowd applauses. Dad introduces the next song.

"Thank you, ladies and gentlemen! This next tune is a family favorite by Dynasty called *Adventures in the Land of Music!*" He then turns to the band and counts them down: "3, 2, 1, hit it!"

The music begins. The crowd is feeling it and Nisa makes a comment, "Oh my God, I love this song!"

"Me too, I'm going to get up and dance, besides, everybody didn't get a chance to see my outfit!" Fatimah says, going out to the dance floor. She catches my father's eye after dancing for a bit, then she two-steps over to our table discreetly so that she does not blow Nisa's cover. Nisa and I catch his eye by raising our glasses to him. Nisa looks over the top of her sunglasses with a wide grin. Dad nearly drops his guitar while singing! He doesn't take his eyes off our table the whole song.

Once the song ends he tells the crowd that the band will take a ten-minute break and motions us to come backstage. We hop up and very smoothly walk backstage to chop it up with my father and the band. We get backstage into the hallway and my father is waiting anxiously with his hands in his pockets.

"Pops!" Nisa calls out to grab his attention. His big smile and hearty laugh invites her over.

"My girls!" he says, opening his arms wide to embrace Nisa first; he pulls her back to remove her shades and see her eyes. Holding her face for a moment, he looks her over and says, "My girl is home!" He hugs her again, then Fatimah, then me.

"Packed house tonight, Daddy!" I say.

"Y'all are killing it out there!" Fatimah adds.

"Oh, we do alright. Why don't y'all come on back and say hey to the fellas?" Dad asks. We agree to that request. Nisa places her shades back on as we walk over to the dressing room.

"Fatimah, will you sing with us tonight… just one? I know you gotta get back to Hakeem and my little grandson," Dad asks.

"Of course, Dad, you got it!" Fatimah answers.

We step into the dressing room to greet the band. "Hey everybody, how y'all doin?" I ask.

We exchange pleasantries for a few moments when "Uncle" Doug has a question for me in particular. "So Jadirah, how are you feeling lately? What's up with Carlos, you know I saw that shit on the internet!" he asks.

"Aww, c'mon now, Doug," says "Uncle" Marvin. "Let's not get carried away."

"No, I ain't judging Carlos but I know his momma! Not everybody is meant to be parents. Ain't no way I would have my wife out there like that. These young boys don't know shit about being a husband… Look! My wife gave me four strong, healthy, intelligent boys. I would work five jobs to keep her happy, she deserves anything she asks for."

"Yeah, I know, she be runnin yo ass like your name was Carl Lewis, nigga!" "Uncle" Joe chimes in jokingly.

"I'm going back to the table," Nisa says, speed-walking away.

"Hey fellas, ahh, Fatimah is going to join us on this next number, okay!" Dad announces.

"Good to see you all!" I say, greeting the group. I wave and seek Nisa.

I begin to worry that we lost our table so I pick up the pace. I go back to the floor, look around and see that we did. Nisa is standing at the bar sipping a martini, looking annoyed that we lost our table. I chuckle to myself and start toward the bar. I sneak up on Nisa.

"So we lost our table?" I say jokingly.

"Yeah, I'm pissed, you want a drink?" she asks.

"Yeah, cranberry juice."

Just then, Dad comes to the stage to begin their second set. The crowd begins to applaud. "Thank you! Thank you! We are glad to be back. We have a special guest back tonight to sing for you. My baby girl, Fatimah!" he says, as the crowd cheers.

Fatimah is the best singer out of all of our siblings. Her voice is velvety and husky all at once. The band begins the first few notes and the crowd begins to cheer. They perform a song called "Love Changes" by Mother's Finest.

I look at my sister as she performs with my father. Music, what a divine expression to watch them perform together, harmonizing and dancing—brings back memories of our childhood. Nisa is rocking side to side, clearly she's over losing our seats. Bringing her has brought me great pleasure. I am experiencing the gift of plenty!

I have to admit, I'm glad Fatimah persuaded me to get out of the house tonight!

TEN

The World is Yours

You know what I love about white folks, y'all? They are loyal to their stylist or barber. Do you know how hard it is to be scrolling down social media and see your clients brag about the $20 blowout they had done in somebody's basement or some $75 box braid job?" I ask from the back seat of the car.

"That's gotta be rough, sis," Fatimah says from the passenger side.

We are silent for a moment. "That's why I sold the shop!"

Fatimah turns all the way around to face me. "Are you for real? You sold the shop! Are you still going to do hair?"

"Yes, well sometimes. Nisa is the new owner."

"That's right!" Nisa states.

"I didn't even hesitate to sign the paperwork."

"Did you tell Carlos yet?"

"No."

"Why are y'all still together, sis? I woulda been gone!" Fatimah asks.

"Cause… we got history? But you know what, me and Carlos are not going to survive on history alone… And in this space that I'm in right now, I don't feel that we have enough to keep going because I'm so tired! Of all the bullshit! I don't want to be sixty fuckin years old with a disconnect notice on our door, cause he fucked the money up! Love and marriage shouldn't always be a struggle!"

"Sis, develop some boundaries, you fail to speak up when you are mistreated. You give away too much of your time! I know you feel like the victim and that's because you are! Fourteen-hour days on your feet with carpal tunnel and chest pain, putting yourself through so much for folks—who will book an appointment with somebody else if you died tomorrow! Wake up! Come out from behind that work station and live! You know what? I want to show y'all something," Nisa says.

"Where are we going?" Fatimah asks.

"Just ride," Nisa replies.

We ride through Germantown and stop at an old warehouse with a large empty lot right next to it. "What are we doing here?" Fatimah asks.

"I wanted to show y'all my new project," Nisa says.

"What are you about to do here?" I ask.

"I'm building a school here. I bought this building and the rowhouses across the street. I wanted to make a real difference. I have a vision for my city and I have a vision for you all too! The world is your oyster."

"This is going to be wonderful, Nisa, taking back the community," I say, looking at the building.

"Well, I know where my baby will be starting school," Fatimah says.

"Let's get back in the car, I better be getting back to the hotel," Nisa says, hopping into the driver's seat.

"Are you good to drive? You and Fatimah had a couple back at the bar," I ask.

"I'm good! The world is ours tonight! Ha ha!" Nisa starts the car.

"A Milli" by Lil Wayne comes on the radio and we begin to rock out in the car! Fatimah raps the lyrics verbatim and Nisa and I are amused by her gangsta. We ride for a while and out of the blue, tipsy Nisa has something to get off her chest.

"Sis, I think you ought to work it out with Carlos, you know he is not a bad guy. He is no good with money but he is not a bad dude, when you think about it," she says.

"Fuck that, he is in her way. She should go," Fatimah adds.

"We support whatever it is that you decide to do," Nisa says.

"Just let me know," Fatimah says.

Having the support is good, knowing that you have what it takes to support yourself is an amazing feeling. I am going to go home and try to make it work with my husband.

ELEVEN

Could I Be Falling In Love

We drop Nisa off at the hotel where she's staying. She goes up to her room in the attire that she started with. On the way to her room, she stops by Tony's room first. She knocks at the door and he answers right away: "Hey."

"Hey."

"Could you meet me in my room in twenty minutes?" Nisa asks.

"Yes."

"Okay, bring your laptop, too. Okay?"

"Alright."

Nisa then goes down to her room and prepares for a shower. She finishes and slips on a black lace nightgown. She applies just a little mist of her favorite perfume. By the time Tony reaches her room, she has a glass of white wine with her sights set on the city of Philadelphia.

There is a knock at the door. Nisa looks out to make sure it is Tony. It is. She lets him in and he immediately assumes that Nisa wants to talk business. "So we have to talk about Wednesday," Tony says, shutting the door.

"What's Wednesday? Remind me?" Nisa asks.

Tony sighs, "The Empowerment Summit."

"Oh, that's right, okay, damn that's right," Nisa says, shaking her head.

"What's wrong? Do you still want to do it or cancel?"

Nisa is silently gazing out of the window at the view of downtown.

"Are you okay? What's on your mind, babe?"

"Jadirah, I think of my poor sister-friend and I have always known her to self-sacrifice. I do the same shit, too!"

Tony is silent. Nisa goes over to her iPad and puts on "Giving You All My Love" by Carl Thomas. Tony walks up to Nisa and takes off her robe to reveal the lace nightgown. Kissing her shoulders tenderly. She asks him: "Why do you want me?"

"Because you are the most amazing woman I've ever met." He then turns her around to face him. "I mean it, Nisa, I want you to be my wife."

Nisa's eyes well up as he kisses her lips gently. Touching. Gently she lays her hands upon his chest and she feels his body tightening. He brings his hands up to her face and slowly slides them down her lingerie to grab her hips. She lowers her gaze for a moment as he draws her closer.

"I am not Jakka. I know a queen when I see one."

She looks relieved. He knows her worth. He kisses her again, passionately devouring her. Controlling the vibe. He is too smooth. Divine masculine energy takes over. Every time she tries to lead, he won't let her and that lights an erotic flame within her. He can hear her deep shuddering breath as the intimacy grows. The kiss goes deeper. He is hungry for her. She tries to rip off his shirt, he grabs her hands and looks her in the eyes, picks her up and places her on the bed. Kissing her neck, she tries to take off his grey sweatpants. He grabs her hands again and places them above her, showing her who's in charge, and it turns her on.

He kisses her body down. He french-kisses her other set of lips until the moans of passion take control of his body. His desire can't wait any longer, neither can hers. Pleasure is awaiting the both of them. He needs this, she responds with warmth from her body. His scent turns her on. She begins to shiver and then she is ready for their bodies to merge. They move together. His thrusts send electricity throughout her body. She doesn't think about Jakka or work. She is free.

Making uninhibited love with the man of her dreams. He is prepared to give her anything she wants. He wants to give her so much.

He continues on thrusting as the panting and moaning goes on. He nibbles on her ear, stroking her breasts tenderly and sweetly. What they share is precious and sacred. In love with one another. No longer feeling imprisoned by a dysfunctional public relationship. She feels safe in Tony's arms. There's no turning back now. Tony makes her forget any pain. This is what sweet love is. Memories won't interrupt what happens now.

TWELVE

Slowly Surely

After I drop Fatimah off at home, I head to my house, hoping to find a common ground or at least achieve an understanding of what we can do with our marriage. I just keep hearing Nisa's voice in my head, "He's not a bad guy." It's ultimately my decision, if I want to stay or not. Carlos and I have years and history between us. Do I want to start over again? Get to know new in-laws again? If I do stay, will it make me look weak? Am I fed up enough? Is Carlos man enough to admit that he has a compulsive buying disorder and that it's ruining everything? He does not want to do the work but he thinks he deserves to be at the top with the hard workers who really want to win.

I can change him, I will go in here and give him an ultimatum.

As my mind races, my fuel light comes on, I realize that we have been driving around the city for hours and I need to stop for gas. As I pull into the gas station pump, my cell phone rings… It's Nisa.

"Hey!" I answer, smiling.

"Hey, where are you?" she says in a low voice.

"At the gas station… why? What's up?" Nisa is silent. "Hello? Nisa?"

"I'm here… I'm going to let myself love Anthony!" she blurts out quickly.

"Good! Congratulations!" I say, grinning.

"Okay. Yep. Call me later and tell me what happened. Tell him that y'all need to go to marriage counseling," she says quickly in a loud whisper. "Okay, I gotta go, bye." She ends the call.

I smile with gratitude. Excited that my very best friend will no longer run from love. Jakka and his "assistant" have humiliated her long enough. Besides, Tony *wants* to be in love. Jakka is madly in love with money. Always has been. He will do ANYTHING for money, Nisa will not. This is what makes Jakka unattractive to her.

After he physically assaulted "Briana" in the threesome months ago for not being "his type," Jakka didn't realize that "Briana's" father was a powerful businessman who had the ability to ruin Jakka for life. So, Jakka had to have "Briana" be his assistant. A cute little blonde who used to be "Brian" years ago.

It's almost like they own him. Nisa told me a while ago that it feels like "Briana" is assigned to him, constantly watching his every move. They are deplorable entertainment folks that deserve one another. One is deceptive and the other is a sad, money-hungry has-been. Jakka is hooked on all types of drugs and cocaine. He pays the price that Nisa is not willing to pay. She will not do whatever it takes. I've always respected her boundaries when it comes to "The Industry."

I pull up to my house with optimism and hope in my heart. I know that it is late, so I'll try not to wake the children.

As I approach the front porch, I notice that the kitchen light is on. Carlos must be awake. Good! I open the front door, immediately I notice the smell of french fries frying. I take off my jacket and set my bag down and toss my keys in the opening of my bag. "Hey," I call out.

"Hey! I'm in the kitchen," Carlos replies.

I head into the kitchen and he doesn't look up. He's cooking fries on the stovetop. I go to sit down on a stool at the breakfast nook.

"Jadirah, we gotta talk," Carlos says very dryly.

"I agree," I reply.

"I spoke to Jakka on the phone earlier today and he told me that Nisa is planning a trip for you and y'all's friends to Dubai… because you need a break? He then advised me to go and Google Anthony's track record to see how privileged I was to even sit in the same room with him because…" Carlos chuckles. "He's a real heavy-hitter in the business world, right! Then after that, he berated me like a child over the college money that I used for investments…"

Carlos is clearly becoming annoyed. I'm not certain where he is going with this but I continue to listen silently.

"Now peep this," Carlos says as he slowly begins moving small batches of fries from the frying pan onto the paper towel-covered plate. "Jakka, my man, my homie! Says to me that… he couldn't fuck with me at all until I get my act together because I hurt his little sis… who is struggling with lung cancer!" Carlos says with a hearty laugh. "Lung cancer!" he says as he turns to look at me as I sit. "My wife kept a secret like lung cancer from me. My wife brought one of the most successful business consultants to see me, to humiliate me into showing an unfinished business plan! I was no way prepared for that sabotage!"

Oh no! I see what he's doing, I think to myself.

"If Ronnie and I had the chance to properly plan a presentation, he could have understood everything!"

I drop my jaw in disbelief.

"And Nisa! Let's talk about Nisa's disrespectful ass. She tried her best to emasculate me and disguise it as concern for our debts and money management. You were sitting right there and didn't defend me, Jadirah!"

My eyes begin to well up.

"You are getting ready to go on a trip to Dubai? Wow! Must be nice. I know that Nisa probably set that up just to spite me! And cancer?" Carlos then turns to face me and I see the anger come across his face. "Cancer! You would keep that from me? What else are you keeping from me, Jadirah? Why do I put up with this? Now I see why niggas leave! But I'm a real man! My kids will have a father! They will have a yard to play in... Shit! I picked this house out! I pay the mortgage! Don't think I didn't see all those comments on the internet, too! All those angry, bitter bitches talkin about how you should leave me cause I'm a scrub and a deadbeat because the truck got took! THAT REPOSSESSION WAS YOUR FAULT! I told you to fill that extra booth at the shop but, nooo! You too damn picky about who you wanna let work in there."

As I sit there listening to Carlos' rant, I begin to think of the rebuttal that I'm going to hit him with.

He continues, "If you do decide that you want to go on your own, just remember this! Who's gonna want you? You got four kids and you're not a spring chicken anymore! A college dropout with a wrinkled belly! What man would go for you with all that baggage? I'll tell you, NO ONE! A sick, worn out, single black woman with four kids? You gotta be shitting me! Don't let Nisa fill your head with all this 'Women Empowerment' bullshit! If you left me, you would be lonely. No one would save you, you are not as pretty as you used to be."

I narrow my eyes at him, then tilt my head to the right and shoot him the coldest look possible. I feel stunned beyond comprehension by what Carlos has to say about me. Maybe I have been keeping secrets, I was trying to avoid him while I was angry. I cannot understand why somehow in his mind I AM THE ONE TO BLAME!

And then it comes to me! This marriage IS all my fault! I have enabled so much, I didn't speak up! He has punished me this whole time! I forced this marriage when I was pregnant with Isaiah! I told him that he didn't need to get me a ring! I told him that we didn't have to have a wedding! I knew he couldn't afford it.

Submission to someone who is not worthy is why we are here at this moment. I wipe the tears from my face and it is clear to me why my next move will have to be for my sanity— more importantly, my self-respect. I slowly begin to stand, searching for the words, breaking out from the state of disbelief that I am in.

Carlos starts up again, calmly. "Now Jadirah, I can see that you're upset and I think that we can work everything out. Okay," Carlos says arrogantly, dismissing facts and actual concerns of mine.

I begin: "Carlos, I wasn't sure if I was going to leave until this moment…" I pause to carefully gather what I want to say. I have so many things to say after such repulsive comments. He honestly believes that I deserve this emotional abuse. "Carlos, I want you to forgive me," I say firmly without emotion. Looking into his face.

Carlos looks confused at first. He then begins to nod slowly in agreement as if I was looking to apologize.

"You can't be what I need you to be. I thought that I could show you how to be a husband if I would just be a good wife and I failed. I, wanted this marriage, you don't want a wife and I see that now! You expected me to be the provider."

He looks at me as if I'm speaking Latin. "What do you mean? Jadirah, if I didn't want to be married, I wouldn't have married you!" Carlos replies, looking to argue.

I choose not to engage to preserve my newfound peace and to not awaken the children. "I'm going to grab some of my things, I'm staying at my sister's tonight. The children are going with my parents tomorrow morning when I come back to get more of my stuff." I begin to walk past him.

Carlos decides to dismiss what I've said. "Yeah, no problem, if you need to clear your head at Fatimah's for a night... I understand. We'll talk in the morning babe, alright?" he says, looking over the top of his glasses in a state of denial, popping a french fry in his mouth.

"No, Carlos, we won't," I say in a serious tone of voice. "Also, as far as secrets go, one thing Jakka left out, I sold Jay's Beauty Salon! I am retired," I say as I started toward the master bedroom to pack my things.

"That's stupid, why would you do that! How are you gonna earn money?"

I don't respond. I continue onward to the bedroom. I begin to pack my items. Carlos comes into the room to ask more questions. "How much did you sell it for? Why did you sell the salon without telling me?"

I zip my book bag with my few items in it and say to Carlos, "I wanted out. I'll see you in the morning."

As I slowly, but surely, start toward the front door, I feel as if there is a weight lifted off my shoulders. I feel free! How Carlos feels is none of my concern anymore. I hear a high-pitched tone as if I am on a different frequency. Carlos is ranting about how much he is owed from the sale of the hair salon. I ignore him. I do not care about him being loyal to me any longer, I don't need his presence in my life. Movement is life. I'm not interested in being a doormat any longer. This toxic marriage has been detrimental to my growth. Carlos is clearly out of his mind to try and play the role of the victim. I, on the other hand, have decided to work on my happiness. No longer will I keep quiet to massage my husband's fragile ego. I step outside and go directly to the passenger side door to place my book bag on the seat.

I have repressed my own desires and needs for so long that I realize I've placed limitations on my own life. I walk over to the driver's side of my car, I take a deep breath and close my eyes. I exhale and open my eyes as I gaze up at the heavens, re-examining my life choices. I close my eyes again for a moment and accept the fact that my next move will not be easy on the kids. Although it will take time to transition, I feel a sense of freedom, the freedom to finally pursue what I want from life.

I will lead. Carlos does not know how to lead. He's been in my way long enough.

I come to a revelation: I'm done… Not angry, not disappointed, and not sad. Just… done.

THIRTEEN

Danger

I just remember thinking, should I kill him? Or should I do something that would really hurt him, really break his heart? All the while, in that yellow cab with the children, trying to hold it together. My face, scraped up and bleeding. I didn't even realize it until the driver noticed and offered me a few napkins. The children kept trying to ask questions. I let them believe that there was some type of accident to save face. I didn't tell them what actually happened until we all got into the house.

That's when I lost it. I began crying hysterically, running around looking for bandages and peroxide to patch my face up. Little David was crying out of control as Isaiah and Ezekiel stood outside the restroom, panicky and agitated, and demanded I tell them what was going on. I opened the restroom door and there they were, my oldest children with concern and panic in their eyes. I didn't hold back, I told them everything. I told them that their father's truck had been repossessed right in front of my salon.

"Taylor and Aliyah, the neighborhood young 'social-media-influencer wanna-be's' happened to be around recording the entire debacle in disbelief; then offered to help me once I started running back into the salon to call you, Mom, Nisa and Carlos!" I say to Fatimah, sitting at her kitchen table, sipping peppermint tea.

"I told them everything, I mean everything," I continue, "I had no idea that they were coming for his truck. I just remember feeling rage! I was livid! I ran into the bedroom closet where he keeps his gun… I found it, it was in a grey metal box… a nine millimeter. I loaded it and had one round ready to go. With tears in my eyes, dirt and blood on my jacket… I then had another bright idea. Destroy his shoes and his clothes! My gears were turning as I took a laundry basket, filled it with all of his expensive designer clothes, dragged it down the stairs while holding the gun with my left hand. The children were hysterical! I was sobbing, the children's voices were muffled and my heart was beating in my ears. I was trembling with anger and I was moving rapidly. I dumped the first load of his beloved clothes on his office floor and started right back up the stairs for more. Cursing and crying, I filled the second load of his precious clothes and sneakers that he cares for so much, that he would never let anything happen to…" I pause. "Fatimah, I watched him clean his sneakers with a toothbrush and I even bought new shoelaces for his Jordans! I pick up his dry cleaning all the time and there I was! Outside of myself and FED THE FUCK UP! There I was, in a rage… I got an idea, I thought it would fix him good! I started laughing, like a psycho! The idea that came to mind was to BLEACH everything! I ran to the laundry room like FloJo, spotted the bleach, took the lid off. I never put the gun down. I ran back upstairs with full intentions of ruining Carlos' clothes and his shoe collection and then my plan was going to be to shoot him!"

Fatimah interrupts, "And that's when I saw you, Sis. I had never in my life seen that look in your eyes. I saw the rage, carelessness, hurt, sadness and insanity all at once. You were holding a gun in one hand and a gallon of bleach in the other. You were a danger to yourself and your children. I hope that you understand that I had to stop you, Jadirah. You had lost it! I thought that you were going to kill him!" Fatimah says lovingly, while grasping my hand.

As I look down into my tea cup, my eyes begin to well up with tears. I nod in agreement with my sister's assessment of my mental state and my reaction of careless emotions after the repossession of my husband's luxury SUV. For a moment in time, I co-existed with an active demon.

"I remember it like it was yesterday," Fatimah reflects. "I said, 'Hey sis' and you stopped! You looked at me and your face was red with bandages all over it and your eyes… your eyes scared me to death! And you stopped, you were walking full speed ahead and the children were terrified!"

"You said, 'Sis, give me the gun. Please, don't do what you were about to do, please Jadirah… Jadirah, look at me.' And when you said my name aloud, that's when I started to feel my right mind return. I slipped away and the demon inside began to decompress."

"That's right! You looked confused at first and tears were streaming down your face. You then looked around at your children and I saw concern in your eyes as I grabbed the bleach from your hand. You then gave a sad smile, the saddest smile I've ever seen at those babies and you started saying, 'It's ok! It's ok, mommy is ok. Okay? Ok, ok, I'm fine. Don't worry.' And that is when I slid on in and took the gun from your left hand. Did you even realize that it was loaded?!?!"

"Yeah I knew, I didn't care! I lost myself. I couldn't believe it. I was outta pocket right in front of little David. How foolish."

"Now, you were upset! I came to the house right on time to help you calm down. When Isaiah called me there was hysteria in his voice. When you called me there was *fury* in your voice!"

"I wasn't aware of how unsafe and unstable my state of mind was in. My heart was beating like a jackhammer and thank God you came over to comfort my children and you took me to Mom and Dad's house. Fatimah, I will always be grateful…" I began to weep, "for you, bringing me out of that dark space."

As Fatimah stands from the kitchen table, I cover my face to sob. She then comes to embrace and comfort me as I weep. Recounting those moments after "The Incident," letting my common sense go and the thought of being so unhinged in front of my beloved children, leaves me ashamed. Ashamed that even good-natured, sweetheart Jadirah would allow a demonic dark energy of pain and destruction to wreak havoc on a household that used to be a peaceful sanctuary for her family and children. I NEVER want to feel that way again. And now I KNOW, I will not EVER feel that way again.

This freedom cry is the best cry I have ever had. I know that I won't ever let myself down the way Carlos did.

As Fatimah releases from our embrace, she grabs a few tissues for me to clean my face. Her husband Hakeem enters the kitchen holding their newborn son, Bilal.

"Your turn, Timah! I wanna talk to my sis," Hakeem says, handing baby Bilal to Fatimah and then sitting across from me at the kitchen table.

Hakeem is a handsome chocolate brother with a well-groomed beard. He grew up in North Philly with us. He went to high school with us and then got sent away for a while for being in the streets. Once he came home, he was the most disciplined Muslim that I've ever seen and he was in love with my sister. He is a respectable man and a very good husband to my sister. Throughout the conversation that Fatimah and I were having, I heard him comforting my fussy infant nephew in the nursery. I know that he has been eavesdropping on us. I don't mind. I would actually like his perspective. I want to know what he thinks about my decision.

"Sis," Hakeem begins. "I would like to know what your plan is. What is your focus right now?" he asks me.

"Well, I see an opportunity to rebuild and get organized. I realize that the divorce is coming on down soon and it will be hard on the children but I'm ready to do it on my own!" I explain.

"I support your decision, Sis, returning to where you left off spiritually—I get it. The 65th Surah is called Divorce for a reason. Sometimes things don't work out, sometimes you grow apart, but you said something that concerns me. You said, 'I'm ready to do it on my own.' I have to ask you if you would just consider making God sufficient for all of your needs. Okay?"

I nod yes.

"Yeah, and you have us! The fam, Nisa just bought the salon, you have a great support system!" Fatimah adds.

I begin to think that my marriage with Carlos has been a facade, maybe it has always been. I take full responsibility. It's a poignant reminder of time wasted. The blessings are four beautiful children and a ton of life lessons. I'm glad to release Carlos from this union of pain.

"What are you thinking about, Sis?" Hakeem asks as I am letting my mind drift off.

"Oh! I was ahhh thinking about the differences in character between a 'husband' and Carlos, what he does possess and what he doesn't possess," I explain, sipping my tea.

"Does he have any examples or role models, mentors that he can, like, look up to?"

"He has my dad. They actually have a good relationship."

"But, I guess I meant, like, foundational family members like uncles, older cousins who are successful husbands. Did he have any idea what it takes to be a man? Let alone become a husband."

Making a good point in his question, I nod slowly. "Wow," I reply, looking at the floor. I bring my eyes up to look at my brother-in-law. "No, he grew up in a crack house. The men he probably saw were either dealers or junkies."

Hakeem is silent.

"He just didn't know how to be a husband, Sis!" Fatimah says.

"No, it's not just that, I saw potential, he wants a family and I know that. Hakeem, lemme ask you something. Do you remember the BMW story?"

"A little, Fatimah told me a little bit about it," Hakeem says.

"Ok, so Fatimah wasn't there so I'll tell you what happened. It was fashion week and Jakkawear was the hottest hip hop clothing line on the market. The fashion show was packed. All of the biggest names in hip hop and R & B were there. The show was a success and the pre-orders had skyrocketed. Well, after the fashion show, there was an after-party that was at the hottest club in New York being thrown for Jakka. Now, mind you, at this time he had the number-one song on the hip hop charts and Nisa was making power moves. They were the "it" couple in the industry at that time. And... I knew that Carlos felt some type of way about them being in the limelight all the time because we used to have our little private conversations. He had always felt ignored by the bigger fashion houses because Jakkawear was considered "urban streetwear." He wanted us to be recognized as an up-and-coming industry couple as well! So he decided to make a statement at the after party. For me, though, it would all be a surprise what he was about to do. My mind was on celebrating my bro Jakka on all of his success. Carlos planned to surprise me with a five-year-old BMW at Jakka's after party in front of everyone!"

"Wait, is that the one you're still driving?"

I raise my eyebrows, closed my eyes, ball my lips in and nod yes. "Now, mind you, Jakka is already a car guy and noticed it was used and then it happened!"

Fatimah begins to chuckle softly.

"Jakka clowned the hell out of Carlos!!" I say, laughing. "He said, 'Yo! You gotta be fuckin kiddin, son! How you gonna be making your kinda money, drivin a brand new Lex Truck, and you gonna gift your shorty a used Beemer? Get the fuck outta here, yo! You really shoulda talked to me first 'Los!' And the party people were lookin out the club window laughing. Our friends who came outside for the big reveal were shaking their heads laughing and Carlos was pissed! So what did I do when I saw the look in his face? I grabbed the key from his hand and said as loud as I could 'Oh my God! Thank you so much babe!' Then I kissed him right on the lips in front of everyone and gave him a hug. Nisa looked right at me while we were huggin it out and she could tell that my reaction was bullshit but the little crowd around us started applauding. That was the best I could do to help him save face. He was quiet the rest of the night.

"I still remember that night like it was yesterday. I knew who he was. I knew he wasn't clear about what the role of a 'husband' is. I knew that he didn't know what he was doing because my dad always had the late model car and Mom kept a newer one, ALWAYS! All of our uncles were the same as Dad. They put their queen and their children ahead of what they wanted. That exchange between Carlos and Jakka, all those years ago…" I pause and took a deep breath "…I even knew back then. Jakka didn't need to shame him or bust him out to expose what type of guy he was. I already knew that he wasn't the type to put family first."

"Wow, okay," Hakeem says. "It makes a little more sense now… his character, you know."

"Right," Fatimah says.

We become silent for a few moments.

"Well Sis, what do you need us to do?" Hakeem asks.

"I need the both of you to help me move my stuff out tomorrow morning. No furniture or anything like that, just clothes, shoes, my beauty basket… stuff like that," I reply.

"Oh okay, and where are we going to take this stuff?" Fatimah asks.

"It's going to a furnished condo that I booked for about a week until I can figure out where my new place should be."

"Okay Sis, we'll help you out on one condition: You make evening prayer with us!" Hakeem says with a smile.

"You got it, I need some prayer!" I say, laughing.

I think that Hakeem and Fatimah have a clear understanding of what is about to happen. We stand from the table to go and prepare for prayer. Fatimah allows me to borrow one of her hijabs. Hakeem is an honorable man, inviting me to pray the evening prayers with them during my time of pain; it will certainly put my heart at ease during this parting taking place with Carlos. The light of prayer has a perfect way of driving out confusion and doubt. It rids me of darkness.

As I began to wash for prayer, I open my heart and empty my thoughts. I accept my blooming, brand new reality. I feel a sense of inner peace. I will begin this new path. I accept the challenge of starting over with no restraints, no fear, no ghosts and no insecurities.

I am ready to go forward. I know that the entire situation has turned into nightmare fuel. I will never return to misery, nor will I submit to merely surviving and suffering to keep peace.

Reborn, yes.

FOURTEEN

Better in Tune with the Infinite

There we stand early that next morning—my father and his pickup truck, my mother, my sister and my brother-in-law—strong and ready to righteously flex on Carlos if he tries to stop me from leaving. It's dark, the sun hasn't risen just yet. It's cool and crisp out with a tinge of fog. I feel empowered with my support system standing by my side.

"Sweetheart, what will you have us do?" Mother asks.

"Will you all come on in and sit in the living room? I want to explain things to the children before they get dressed and go with you and dad," I reply in a low soft tone.

"You got it, honey, whatever you want us to do. Okay? We are here for you," Dad says.

I nod and we all start toward the house. I unlock the door and notice that the entire house is still asleep. I suddenly receive a call from Nisa. I answer on the second ring.

"Hey, good morning, Sis," I say.

"Hey beautiful! Did y'all work things out last night?" Nisa asks quietly.

I close my eyes and sigh, "No, we didn't, I'm at the house now with the fam. I'm about to move out."

"WHAT!? Wait a minute, what happened?"

"I can't talk right now, Sis, I'll explain everything later."

"I'm comin' over there right now!" Nisa says firmly.

"No! Sis, please. What if some neighbors or bloggers see you and put it on social media?"

Nisa is silent for a moment. "Fuck that, I'm on the way," she replies dryly before hanging up.

I sigh and roll my eyes.

"Was that Nisa?" Fatimah asks.

"Yes, she's on her way. I guess she doesn't care about her image or her brand right now." We all become silent for a moment. "Well, I'd better get the children up so that I can get everything ready," I explain to the group.

As I march up the stairs, I notice the stench of stale marijuana smoke in the hallway. I smile as I shake my head. Carlos must have felt bold last night about not sticking to the rules of not smoking in the house or around the children. I go into Isaiah and David's room first. I give them both a gentle nudge to wake them, along with a kiss on the cheek. Once they've awakened, I instruct them to go and brush their teeth and wash up quietly.

I go into Ava's room and do the same. Ezekiel is last. I peek into the master bedroom and Carlos is in a deep slumber. I quietly shut the door, and instruct the children to meet me in Isaiah's bedroom to talk. I feel a calmness about the energy that my children have collectively. I wonder if they see things as I have recently.

Once everyone is finished with their hygiene process, we exchange morning pleasantries and greet one another as we settle down quietly and take our seats. I begin as I sit down at Isaiah's computer desk and place myself in the swivel chair:

"Ok everyone, so I have to tell you what will be happening today. You all will be spending the day with Grandma and Grandpa. Mommy has a lot of business to handle today and your grandparents are going to look after y'all today," I explain.

"Mommy, where are you going to be today?" Ava asks.

"Well, I'm going to come right on out and just say it," I say reluctantly. "I am moving out today. I'll be moving into a temporary residence, until I can find my own place."

"Are you and Daddy breaking up, Mommy?" David asks innocently.

I sigh and answer my youngest child, "Yes, sweetheart."

The disappointment in his eyes makes me feel like I have just ruined his poor little life. I wish I could've said something better. I can't give them anything but the truth, no matter how much it hurts.

"We understand, Mom," Isaiah chimes in.

"We get it, we ain't stupid," Ezekiel says.

"Mommy, I'm going to miss you!" Ava says sadly.

"No you are not, because I will be seeing you every day. When I get my own place, you all will have a room and your father and I will work something out. Okay?"

"I think that everything is going to be alright, Mom," Isaiah says, reaching for a hug from me. We embrace.

"Everything is going to be fine. Okay?" I say, looking all of my children in their faces.

The children follow my instructions and begin to prepare to leave with my parents. This is really happening. I have earned this moment. As I start down the stairs, I hear Hakeem and my father talking.

"What's up, y'all?" I ask curiously.

"Well, honey," my father begins, "Hakeem and I were just talkin' about how we should probably be the ones to reinforce your plans to Carlos so that he's clear that you are serious about this move. He should not be kept in the dark, that wouldn't be fair, let alone wise."

"I told him last night, he didn't want to accept it, Dad," I state. I feel in this moment that I'll agree to whatever is easiest. I want the energy to stay calm. I'm not in the mood to overthink. I am ready to go and I feel it in my soul! "I'm fine with that, Dad, let's just try to keep the noise down so that he can awaken naturally. I don't know what to expect once Nisa arrives. Fatimah, we can start in the master closet first, okay?" I say urgently.

"Sure," Fatimah answers.

Hakeem has agreed to help move the packed boxes and bags to my father's pick-up truck. Isaiah and Ezekiel are the first to be dressed and surprisingly have asked if they can help Hakeem and Dad. This warms my heart so. They get it, they understand.

I agree to let them help, they are strong and athletic and with their helping hands, this will cut moving time in half. My sons' willingness to help me move out shows me that maybe they've been silently observing our dysfunction and just maybe they've seen enough and want me to get away. I don't feel judged by my children at all. I'm grateful for their wisdom.

Fatimah and I begin in the master closet. My sister doesn't ask questions, she just starts packing. Fatimah packs the first duffel bag hurriedly, and she is indeed efficient, wasting no time because it is a bit uncomfortable knowing that Carlos is asleep in the next room. My sister is swift. We do not talk. Within minutes we are downstairs with four bags packed with clothes and shoes. My mother announces that she will put Ava and little David in her car and head home. I agree to her plan. As my mother reaches for her keys in her purse, she looks at me with a slight smile and then… her eyes draw right past me as the smile goes to her jaw slightly dropping.

I take a deep breath and close my eyes for a moment. I know that Carlos has awakened and he is behind me.

"Good morning, Carlos," my mother says.

"Mornin, Mrs. Diane. What's the problem? What's going on?" Carlos asks.

I turn around. My first impulse is to explain everything. The expression on Carlos' face is of genuine confusion.

"We are all here to help Jadirah move out, peacefully, Carlos," Fatimah explains.

I turn to Carlos, "We spoke about this last night. The children are going to Mom and Dad's today," I remind Carlos of my decision.

"Wait, you really leavin'? Y'all were just gonna help her sneak out while I was sleeping? That's fucked up!" Carlos says.

In that moment I turned to my mother and say, "Why don't we get them in the car now, Mom," I open the front door as Carlos begins to rant with rising anger.

My father approaches Carlos to get him to calm down, explaining that this is "Jadirah's decision" and that it's all for the best. I start outside down the stairs with my mother to secure the children in her car. I tell them that I love them and I let them know that everything will be okay. As I watch my mother pull off and drive away, I pull out my phone and my earphones. I know what song I want from my playlist that will straighten my mood out. I select Jay Electronica, better in tune with the infinite for my soul on this early-morning life transition. I hit play to get into my zone.

I take a deep breath and head back into the house. I look up and notice Isaiah and Ezekiel are carrying boxes marked "Linens & Towels;" I smile as they pass me. They both glance at me with a look of reassurance. I feel their support and I'm shocked at how quickly Fatimah has packed half the linen closet! I walk right past Carlos, my father and Hakeem and go right back up the stairs to my busy, determined sister. She's packing my small dresser now.

She notices me as I enter the room. "Sis, pull your toiletries bag and pack it and put what you are going to wear tomorrow and your pajamas and stuff in this bag that I pulled and sat over there," Fatimah says, pointing to the dark grey and black duffel bag to the right of her.

I oblige. I am in awe of my baby sis as she neatly folds my clothing and quickly packs it all away.

She has known for quite some time that I deserve better. I thought that I would feel anxious or edgy about today's move; instead I feel strong and confident. I do not feel sadness at all. My father, the man that I respect the most in this world, is here with me and he's got my back! I pack my duffel bag as Fatimah has instructed. It is to ride with me in my car.

I head back downstairs and Hakeem is with Carlos on the front porch now with a passionate conversation. I don't care. I don't even look over at them. My father and my sons are securing packed boxes on Dad's pick-up truck.

Just as I hit the unlock button on my keys to pop my trunk open, Nisa pulls up. Tony is driving. Nisa hops out and she's dressed in sweats and a silk scarf tied neatly around her hair. She starts right toward me. Her arms reaching for a hug, concern and love in her eyes, we embrace. A tight embrace, so tight it pulls my right earphone down. Now I hear Carlos loud and doing his very best to make a scene.

"She's my wife! Whatchu talkin' about, Hakeem? It's really simple, bro. Me and her are in this together and she ain't going nowhere!" Carlos cries out.

"Carlos, if she's ready to go, you can't make her stay, brother, her mind is made up," Hakeem explains.

"Sis," Nisa begins as we release from the supportive embrace. "What do you need me do?" Nisa says firmly and intensely… Looking directly into my eyes with all seriousness.

"Go find Fatimah, she's in my old room," I say with a wink. I smile, "Fatimah is in charge of this whole thing, Sis." Nisa smiles and nods.

Meanwhile, Carlos is on the front porch jumping around and yelling in protest like a drunken troglodyte. Nisa approaches the stairs leading to the house and Carlos then notices her approach, then directs his anger to her.

"There you are! It's you, right? You told her to leave me, Nisa! This is yo fault!" Carlos says angrily.

"What? Nigga please. I tried to get her to stay with you and work it out! This is all her decision! Wussup, Keem, Timah in here?" Nisa replies.

"Yeah, she's upstairs with Pop and the boys," Hakeem says.

"So you here to help her move out, right? Nisa, look at me!" Carlos says.

"Well I certainly didn't come here to waste my time! I'm here to support Jadirah," Nisa replies, walking through the front door into the house.

I open the back door of my car to place a few immediate items that I'll need for the next few days. I begin to feel lighter emotionally. We are in the process and I feel that all of this wasn't as bad as I thought it would be. Maybe it's a good thing that I managed my expectations before we all began this morning. Maybe that humiliating repossession *was* the spark. Even though I was at my lowest point, God has brought me through it and is bringing me to a new mindset.

The Most High has the ability to change the most hopeless situation into the best paradigm shift I have ever experienced. I am hopeful, no longer silent… Sometimes I was just silent, silent because of exhaustion. I had convinced myself that my silence would keep peace around my marriage.

Whose peace was I protecting? Carlos? Being silent cost me *my* peace of mind long enough. I am done holding on. Holding on for what? Holding on to what? I want to go on my own. I don't ever want to check with Carlos before I make a decision. I will do what needs to be done, the right way!

I'm through financing his recklessness. I think back to about a month ago. I was about to sit down and pay the salon's utility bills when suddenly, a notification came through on my smartphone. My bank app sent me an alert that my account had been overdrawn $6.81. I immediately suspected fraud or identity theft, since I knew that I had enough in my account to pay my bills. Before I could even completely log in to check my account activity, Carlos called me to apologize about an online purchase he made and how he'll pay me back when he gets his paycheck. Well, those types of surprises are now gone forever! So many scars, tears, sleepless nights, past due bills, insecurities and disappointments… all to be able to say, "Yeah, I'm a real one." A real what? A real fool? A real doormat? A real ride or die chick? A real emotional punching bag for a selfish, unstable little boy pretending to know how to be a man?

No longer will I be punished for loving him. And shockingly, I don't regret what we've shared. I've learned so much. Now, it is time for me to move on. I have to go! I'm too fly for this shit!

My music has me focused. I feel a gentle tap on my shoulder. I turn around from arranging my bags in my car and see my father motioning for me to remove my earphones. I comply.

"Hey sweetheart, that's everything. Fatimah said that we're all finished here, okay?" Dad says, reaching for a hug. "Are you alright, Jadirah?" he asks, releasing from the embrace.

"I am now, Daddy, thank you so much," I say as I watch his eyes well up with tears.

I know that he is proud. My two eldest boys come to give me hugs as they prepare to leave with my father. Fatimah and Hakeem are already sitting in their car. I notice that some of the neighbors have come outside to check out the scene. How could they not? Carlos was boisterous during the entire process.

"Whenever you're ready, Sis!" Nisa says, hopping into the passenger side of her luxury Bentley.

I nod at her and take one last look at Carlos on the front porch, dressed in his slippers and night clothes. He is frowning at me and shaking his head, I sigh. I shrug my shoulders. As I look down to open the driver's door, I am greeted by Lil Bit and my mother-in-law.

"Good mornin, how you doin?" Lil Bit asks while walking up to my car.

"Mornin," I reply dryly.

"Well, where is everybody goin? What's goin on?" my mother-in-law, Ms. Bev, asks, looking at my father's car and at Carlos on the porch.

"I'm moving out! You all have a blessed day," I smile at them both as I hop in my beat-up Beemer and lead the caravan to my temporary residence.

Carlos stands on the porch fuming with anger as his guests approach him. "She left you?" Lil Bit asks. Carlos nods yes.

"To hell with her then, ol' high-yellow bitch, thinkin she better than everybody else. What the hell she know about takin care of a husband anyhow? Shit, you wasn't happy with her ass anyway. She wasn't makin enough bread to be havin no husband anyway! She think she Diane? Her momma ass think she white, stayin home, lazy homemaker. Shit, they spoiled yellow bitches. Black women need to work two jobs if they have to, to keep they man happy! You don't need her baby. Momma is here, let's go in the house. You my son, that lazy bitch is good for nothin nohow!" Ms. Bev says as the three of them go inside.

With a confused look on his face, Carlos knows that things are going to be different.

FIFTEEN

Nakamarra

I thought I wouldn't be able to do it. Even in the past, when I would try to go, something would always pull me back. I started to actually believe that I had no way out.

As I watch my support system move my bags into the extended residence, I begin to feel lighter. My spirit is at peace and I begin to feel that a part of me is beginning to unlock. The old go-along-to-get-along Jadirah is fading away.

What is this energy that is emerging? Is it self-determination? Liberation? I thought I'd feel sad. I don't. I feel optimistic about the future. Even with lung cancer, four children, and temporary housing, I feel optimistic about my plans. I stand at the doorway of the fully furnished condo, watching my loved ones work hard for me. It's only 10:09 a.m. and we've done so much. Even Tony has pitched in to help out. I step outside to look around. I take a deep breath and I feel grateful and blessed. I look up and notice a beautiful hawk flying above me.

"Hey Sis, whatcha doin?" Nisa asks, approaching from behind me.

"I'm looking at this hawk, flying high," I answer. "It's so close to us."

"You know that in some cultures when a hawk comes close like this, it could mean that the universe wants you to speak your truth. To learn powerful lessons or preparing you for leadership. You know, spiritually maturing, clairvoyance and things like that," Nisa says while observing the hawk.

"Is that right? Well the timing is accurate!" I say, smiling.

"Look, okay… I want everyone to come to brunch at the hotel where we're staying. Okay?" Nisa says in a no-nonsense manner.

"Okay, that's fine. I don't have anything going on today."

"Oh yes, you do! You got a lot going down today!" Nisa says with a smile and a wink, as she turns to walk back into the condo.

Everyone finishes up and I instruct them to not unpack anything. I will not be staying here long. I plan to buy my own house very soon. Dad announces that he will be joining us after he drops the boys off at his house.

We arrive at the hotel where Nisa and Tony are staying for a very private celebration in a secluded space. Fresh and neat, complete with fresh flower arrangements as centerpieces atop a long rectangular table with a white tablecloth. I love fresh flowers in any season. Carlos would never send me flowers. He would always say that it's a waste of money and they're gonna die anyway. Oh well, it's a thing of the past now.

Nisa lets out a long breath as we were being seated. "That should be enough for one day!" Nisa sighs.

"I agree, Sis," Fatimah adds. "A great deal has been accomplished here this morning."

"Good work everyone, I want to say that I'm very proud of you all but in particular… Jadirah, baby, you stayed calm and sharp throughout the whole ordeal. I mean you kept your composure, we got everything done and then we split, jack!" my father adds, smiling.

"Well, you all should know that I'm beyond grateful for everything, I truly am, Daddy. I told myself to remain level-headed, don't overreact and this all will soon be a memory," I reply.

"I dig that! It could have been a nightmare, especially for my grandbabies. I'm just glad it's all over," Dad says.

"Amen to that!" Fatimah adds.

The waiter comes to our table and begins to take my father's order first. My father orders black coffee only. He hasn't eaten breakfast in years. Nisa is amused that he is still so disciplined.

"Pops, you still don't eat breakfast? After all these years?" Nisa asks lightheartedly.

"No, I do not," Father replies.

"Still one meal a day?"

"That's right, between the hours of four and six."

"Do you snack?" Tony asks.

"No snacks and I'll only drink black coffee or water. I may snack on crackers or take a few bites of fruit if I am traveling," Dad explains.

"Wow, that must take a lot of willpower and restraint," Tony adds.

"Pops has been eating like that for as long as I remember," Nisa says.

The waiter continues to take drink and food orders as I think about how sharp and disciplined my father still is after all these years. He was poisoned before back in the day when he was a musician. It put him in the hospital for a few days. He wasn't ashamed for being a Muslim, but sometimes his pride made him a target for the ones who were Islamophobic. In those days, he received lots of hate and death threats when he was on the road. He was fearless. He became a successful professional musician and the struggle turned him into a wide-awake, sharp and disciplined man. He'll only eat my mother's cooking. I'm sure that now, with my newfound freedom, I'll be as fearless and successful as my father whom I adore so much.

After our orders are all placed, we all begin a little small talk, glancing at our smartphones from time to time. Nisa speaks of the awards show that she and Jakka were invited to that she is excited to attend. Fatimah and Hakeem speak of being new parents, the love and joy of parenthood along with the sleep deprivation that comes with it. Tony speaks of upcoming business ventures and politics.

As the ordered brunch meals begin to arrive, I move to sit up in my chair and feel a sharp pain in my chest and back. I close my eyes tightly and take a deep breath. I open my eyes and look at Fatimah seated to my right, and she is staring hard at me.

I look around for a moment to see if anyone else in our group noticed. I tried to be inconspicuous. Fatimah won't take her eyes off of me. I know that she is concerned.

She whispers to me, "Sis, are you alright? When do you start chemotherapy?"

I shake my head. "I'm fine, Sis, I go soon. Let's enjoy this food, man, it looks good!" I say, smiling.

As I consume my meal, I begin to think of how I'll break one last secret to Nisa and Fatimah before Nisa departs to the airport.

Once we all finish our meals, Nisa excitedly pays the bill and eagerly requests that we all get back together again this way very soon. We exchange grateful pleasantries as we begin to exit the private eating space. I ask Nisa if Fatimah and I could help her pack for her departure. She says yes, and we start on our way to her hotel suite. I watch my beloved sisters chat as we walk down the hotel hall. I'm in awe of my youngest sister and her display of strength and tenacity this morning in support of my exodus. I admire her.

I then glance over at my boss-ass sister-friend Nisa with a smile on my face, thinking of all the obstacles she has overcome. She has so much to give and offer. She's worked with the biggest names in the fashion and entertainment business. Her passion has made her into a mogul and she is in town to check up on lil ol' me.

I'm surrounded by authenticity; they are my support system committed to pick me up and put me back into the driver's seat.

We approach Nisa's suite and enter the room one at a time. It smells like Issey Miyake women's fragrance. Fatimah notices lingerie on the ground. "Uh oh! Looks like somebody got lucky last night, Sis!" Fatimah says, laughing.

"Sure did! It was essential and it was amazing. I didn't think I could feel like that ever again. I didn't want him to stop," Nisa adds, giggling.

"I knew you were in love again, Nisa," I say.

"Yeah," Nisa pauses. "And I know that you were having chest pains at brunch earlier."

I drop my jaw and look at her.

"Don't say nuthin! I know, I don't always speak on it but I peep everything, sis. When are you going to start chemo? Cause, that's the next order of business now that you're on your way back to being independent."

"Soon, don't worry about it," I reply, looking at my smartphone. I squint my eyes and wrinkle my brow. Carlos is calling. I decline the call.

"So, what time do you all have to be at the airport, Nisa?" Fatimah asks while folding Nisa's clothing to be packed.

"Whenever I'm ready! We are using the private plane on business," Nisa adds boastfully.

"I know that's right," Fatimah murmurs.

My phone begins to ring again. It is Carlos, eager to speak to me, I presume. I decline the call again and place my phone on vibrate. "I need some music. Can we work to music?" I ask.

"I got you! I'm in the mood for some Motown. Are y'all cool with that?" Nisa says, searching her playlist.

"Yeah that's the vibe."

"I'm cool with that!"

The music starts and I begin to place Nisa's folded clothes into her suitcase. We all fall silent while we vibe to the music for a few minutes, and then I begin to receive notifications of several text messages.

They are all from Carlos. What a big surprise, I think to myself. I sit down at the desk, preparing to be amused at what he has to say about my departure. I begin to read the text messages and I become curiously entertained by what he has texted. I find it funny, and then I feel justified. His take on me leaving has left him sounding like a delusional narcissist. I begin to shake my head as I raise my eyebrows and ball up my lips.

Fatimah notices my body language. "Sis, what's up?" she asks.

"Carlos sent me a whole book of a text, girl, he's nuts! Read this!" I say as I stand up from the chair, handing Fatimah the phone.

Fatimah takes the phone and begins reading the text messages. Her eyes are narrowed as she draws the phone to her face to continue reading. Then, her jaw drops.

"Oh hell naw!" Fatimah says aloud.

"What is it?" Nisa asks from the kitchen area.

The venom comes from Fatimah's voice. "Girl, Carlos is just ridiculous! Lemme read this bullshit to you." Fatimah begins to read:

"Jadirah, I cannot begin to tell you how disappointed I am in you for pulling that fiasco so early in the morning. What is the matter with you? Have you lost your mind? You just had to make a scene in front of our kids didn't you? You need to get yourself together and ask yourself some tough questions, because I don't know what it is that you want. I don't hit you and I don't cheat and you wanna leave? There are plenty of women out here that would love the chance of being with me. So I'll give you a week to figure out what it is that you want to do. Just understand this, the doors of reconciliation will begin to close soon, so once you pick a side you will need to stay right there! If you wanna fight, I'll give you one. I'm not giving up my house and you can't have the kids. Fuck it! No alimony either! You will need to do it all on your own! I'm tired of you trying to play the victim. I can't believe that you would want to break up the family. You are a selfish crybaby and you need to give me half of the money that you sold the shop for. I'll be waiting for your apology."

"Oh my GAWD!" Nisa exclaims, widening her eyes. "Is he for real?"

"Serious as a heart attack," I say dryly.

"This fool is ridiculous. I'm gonna text him back," Fatimah says.

"No! Don't!" I say, snatching the phone from Fatimah.

"Man, fuck this nigga, Carlos! He is so self-involved and clearly his head is so far up his ass he can't even be accountable for everything falling apart! It's all his fault!" Nisa adds.

"Well sis, it needed to… everything needs to fall apart. It wasn't built with a strong foundation to begin with. I'm in a position now that I can rebuild the right way," I say. "He said some of the most horrible shit to me last night, I won't repeat it, ever. He showed me who he truly was and made me feel like anything that happens that is bad is all my fault. He resented me and this marriage. And all I could do was sit there like 'damn, I gotta go.' Then, peep this… I started thinking, I have women who are clients who come in and don't have no conversation, no personality, they don't pray, they don't cook, don't clean, terrible hygiene, don't read, just empty airheads. All they are is cute and thick. All they do is twerk on the pole all night, put anything in their mouths for money, get high and drunk, shop all day, get their lashes done and then come and see me for their sew-in and frontal install. These niggas come in and drop hundreds on their bundles and give even more cash for their shopping habits! And here I am, with 12- to 14-hour work days on my feet, back killing me, hands cramping up, I pray all day long, went to etiquette school, I cook, I clean, I'm polite, educated, funny, I pay charity and do good deeds, and what do I get!?! A fly-ass nigga who won't even send me flowers, let alone hand me $500 dollars to go shopping, take me to dinner or get a massage appointment at the damn spa! I'm not worth it? But these ignorant hoes are worth it?"

My eyes begin to well up as I look down and shake my head. Nisa and Fatimah are silent at my emotional venting. "I'm not going to give Carlos the satisfaction of a response. He will just get divorce papers!"

"Hell yeah!" Fatimah says excitedly.

"You will have the best legal team that money can buy, sis, and as for that shit about all of the THOTS that come to see you… don't envy those girls for one second. You don't see what they have to put up with to get what they get. Trust me! Some men don't think that it's not worth anything if they don't pay money for it and people who are built like that suffer the worst. Just think about it, Carlos would have probably loved you the right way if you mistreated him and made him feel small! It's a mindset, I see it all the time. You can't talk butterfly language with caterpillar people," Nisa says.

"Boom, and let the church say amen, Nisa! Good Lord, that's the truth," Fatimah says, laughing.

Nisa reaches toward me for a sisterly embrace. "We got you Sis, you alright? You are going to rebuild, the right way. Now, let's pack so we can get going!"

Nisa has asked Fatimah and I to see her and Tony off to the airport as they head to New York. We tell her we will go. We finish packing everything and go down to the lobby ahead of Nisa. With effort, I try my best to clear Carlos' text messages from my mind. I feel disgust for this man that I was once madly in love with. I've tolerated enough. It is easy to wish that all of this could have been avoided. I felt that deep down inside it would eventually lead to this. I've tried to leave several times. I've tolerated varying degrees of narcissistic behavior for so long, I just accepted it as normal. I would just remain silent, to cope, to survive. Sometimes I was just silent because of exhaustion. I had convinced myself to hold on because of our history. No longer is it a good excuse to remain miserable.

Fatimah and I walk into the hotel lobby and we notice Tony checking out at the front desk. He notices us and smiles and nods to us. We take our seat and make small talk as we wait for Nisa to arrive. I'm glad that she has invited us to see them off. I love Nisa. I don't know if I would have gotten through the weekend without her support. I glance over at Fatimah and she chats with Tony and I am grateful.

That powerful blooming feeling is rising up in me again. It feels like spiritual maturity. Is it contentment? Maybe it's courage! I don't know what it is. I'm on the precipice of something bigger than I know.

Nisa arrives, looking fabulous as ever in her signature shades and fire engine red matte lipstick. She's dressed in all black, down to her suede stilettos. Fans begin to crowd around while we wait for the valet to bring her car around. She takes selfies with them joyously. She's always kind to her fans. The car pulls up and we hop on into the back seat. Tony drives.

"Man, this car is so beautiful," I murmur, looking around the car as we sit inside.

"You like Bad Boy, Jadirah?" Nisa says, smiling as the valet opens her door.

"Yes, it's beautiful and it smells so nice in here."

"Well, I'm glad that you approve, because it's *yours*! Here is your title. No payments. Happy Birthday!" Nisa says, grinning, handing me a folder with paperwork inside.

"No way!" Fatimah gasps.

"I, I… oh my goodness! What!?"

Nisa begins to laugh. "Yes, I've watched you struggle driving that beat-up Beemer your whole adult life. I had to pull rank and upgrade you!"

"Thank you so much!"

"We've been test driving it all weekend, we knew you would love it," Tony says while driving.

"You deserve the very best, Sis. I just love you so much," Nisa says, holding my hand.

"You're going to make me cry," I say, closing my eyes tightly.

"You better not cry, then I'll start crying!" Fatimah adds.

Nisa begins to talk about all of the features of the car and how she got such a great deal on it because Jakka is friends with the owner of the dealership. I am astonished and shocked at this luxury gift. The girls at the salon are not going to get over this one!

We arrive at the airport and I have been waiting for the right time to reveal some news that I've been holding for some time now. When Tony hops out to check in with the pilot of the G4, I decide to tell them about what I've been hiding.

"Hey you guys, I need to tell you both something and you can't speak to anyone about it. Promise?"

"Yeah sure."

"Of course, no problem. What's up?"

I take a long deep breath as I close my eyes to reveal my secret. "You know how when we were little we said if we hit it big that we would never say so? We would just say 'I had an investment that worked out.' You know?"

"Yeah, so… what's your point?" Nisa says, scrolling her smartphone, distracted.

"OH MY GAWD!! It's you! Oh Jadirah, it's been all over the news!" Fatimah says loudly.

"Shhhh don't say the words!"

"What is going on, I'm lost! What's been on the news? I've been on a whole 'nother side of the planet!" Nisa asks.

"Jadirah hit the number for one hundred and fifty mill…" Fatimah starts to explain as I interrupt her aggressively.

"Shut your damn mouth! Do not tell Mommy, y'all don't tell anyone, please! If Carlos found out… Shit if his people found out… the kids would be kidnapped and God knows what else! You got it!?!" I say, frightened.

"Jesus, Jay! You're shaking. Just calm down, we will not tell a soul. I can't believe you've been holding this in all this time," Nisa says in a calm, nurturing tone. "Now that you got this kind of money, fearlessness, fearlessness, fearlessness. Just like Grandma said!"

"Yes!! And I understand about Carlos and his shady-ass people. They will try and pull you into all types of schemes. I promise not to say anything to anyone, Sis," Fatimah says as she reaches for a hug. "I am so proud of you!"

We embrace.

The three of us sit there in silence for a moment. Reflecting. What a weekend. What an outcome!

Tony comes to open Nisa's door as their visit comes to a close. We have some more small talk as we exchange parting pleasantries. As Nisa begins to board the private jet, she blows a kiss to us, then waves. Then she tilts her sunglasses to the tip of her nose and nods slowly, reminiscent of the confident nod she gave me back in court all those years ago, when we were just kids. I look at Fatimah and smile. I look at my new luxury birthday gift in pure amazement. I guess my due season has bloomed. I will receive any blessings with open arms.

Prototype

I see your hair is thickening back up!" Tina says excitedly, trimming my shorter tresses.

"Right! I'm so glad it just thinned out some, after chemo treatments," I reply.

"We really miss you around here, Jadirah, it was only three months ago that you stopped working in here. Do you miss working? Are you bored at home?"

"I never stopped working, I retired from styling hair but I am still working on several different projects, as a matter of fact!" I reply in a sassy way, as Tina rotates the styling chair to face her.

"Okay, so what types of projects, sis?" Tina asks, lowering her voice so that the rest of the customers in Jay's Beauty Salon can not hear our conversation.

I sigh, "Well, let's just say I'm a venture capitalist, Tina, and that's about all I can say." I shrug my shoulders and raise my eyebrows.

"Okay, so is that why you sold this shop?"

"No, I sold Jay's Beauty Shop because I wanted to start over. It was a personal decision. I had to become receptive to movement and letting go of everything, including this shop, which was a part of my spiritual release. I needed to be free!" I say to my former co-worker and personal stylist.

"Girl, that's deep! I can see your growth and I can tell that you've been turning into sister Iyanla," Tina says, laughing after pulling the comb-out cape off of me, finishing my haircut.

I chuckle a bit at Tina's "fun shade" and hand her double the cost for my salon service. Tina quickly notices that I've handed her more than what the service is priced for.

"Sis, you need change?" Tina asks.

"No ma'am, that's all you! I love it! Thank you so much," I say, standing from the hydraulic chair.

"I appreciate you, Jadirah," Tina says, reaching for a hug.

We embrace. We say our goodbyes and I make my way to my car. I'm in a hurry to get to the supermarket because I have to be back home by four o'clock. That is when Carlos will be dropping the children off at my house.

I check my phone after I start the car. I have text messages from the usual crew. Nisa, Ava, Mom, the lawn care guy Mr. Joe, and, of course, Carlos. I read Carlos' text first because he has the children. "Jay, I should be out to your crib in an hour," it reads.

"Okay, thanks!" I text back and send.

As I sigh and place my smartphone into my bag, I feel gratitude seep into my spirit for my newfound peace with Carlos, now that we are officially divorced. It was a rough three months; he wanted a fight and I let him have everything I left behind. Our battle wasn't for material things. We had a custody battle on our hands. No alimony or child support. I don't need a damn thing from him. We were in court over our children. We agreed on joint custody and then I shocked the hell out of him when I closed on my house out in Devon all the way in Chester County! Blew his mind!

He thought Nisa and Jakka bought my house for me. They didn't. All me! A classic Georgian Revival Mansion with the grandeur of estates in the early 1900s. Nine bedrooms, nine bathrooms, a courtyard, five-car garage and a swimming pool that has been masterfully updated. I moved out there for Grandma Faye. She was a housekeeper for the wealthy white families out there where she was tasked not only for housekeeping but cooking as well.

I decide to call Nisa in my car, but first, my playlist selection is the one thing on my mind. "So the Lox, Mary, Denzel Curry or Gregory Porter?" I ask myself aloud. "Gregory Porter it is." I make my selection of smooth music to ride to on my way to the health food market as I prepare to call my sister-friend, Nisa.

I make the call then turn my music down. "Sis!" Nisa answers on the second ring.

"Hey beautiful, I missed your call! What's goin on? You ready for tonight?" I ask.

"Yes! This is the last appearance I agreed on with Jakka. I'm both exhausted and excited. Did I tell you I'm wearing a custom Valentino gown? Emerald green!"

"Well, of course it needs to be green! Wouldn't be caught dead in red!" We start laughing at our little Wiz inside joke.

"You know why I will always love green, right?"

"How could I ever forget? Those early years, those green Cortez Nikes."

"Yeah, green represents life! But for real, it reminds me of where I started. Grimey Philly! The origin, you know what I'm sayin'! I'll never forget, I'm so Philly! But that's not why I called. I wanted to know how things were going out there in Devon. Are you used to the WASP watching you all the time?" Nisa asks slyly.

"Actually it's not that bad, not as bad as when Grandma used to work out here. It's more diverse than I expected. There are a couple families who won't even look at me, though."

"Prejudice," Nisa interrupts.

"Yeah but I don't give a damn. I'm living my truth. You feel me? And, if my truth offends you then that's your problem, not mine!" I say firmly.

"Say word."

"How are you and Jakka gonna deal with the gala tonight?"

"It'll be cool, we know how to keep up the appearance of contentment but the reality is… I let go of everything that was expected of me. Jakka respects my decision. I'm grateful that he understands."

"Good. Friends!"

"Friends for life! Oh yeah, I wanted to tell you. I'm expecting!"

"Shut the front door!" I say, shocked.

"Yes! Tony and I are expecting! I can't believe it, girl, we are 40!"

"I know right! This is a blessing, sis." I pull into the market parking lot.

"I gotta go but I'll call you later after the gala. Okay? I love you, Jadirah!"

"I love you too, congratulations! Peace!"

I end the call and park way in the back so that I may walk a bit through the parking lot to enjoy the nice summer sunshine. I do my best to conceal my excitement for Nisa's new life. What a blessing! I'm so excited for the both of us, grateful for the awakening even at forty years old. Changing your life and finding freedom while you're still fly.

I walk into the store to grab a shopping trolley. I suddenly change my mind and grab a basket instead. I have to keep in mind that Carlos is on the way to my house and I don't have time to big shop.

I notice that they've rearranged the produce section and I become instantly annoyed. I grab the fruits and lettuce for the tacos that I will be preparing for tonight with the children. "Okay, almond milk and cereal. Don't forget the mineral water," I mumble to myself. I gather the items in my shopping basket and I step in line.

The line is long, I shake my head and sigh. The elderly lady behind me says, "Well, geez! With a checkout line this long you would think that they'd open another lane!"

"Well, why would they do that? That would make no sense whatsoever!" I reply in a wise guy manner. The line erupts in laughter at my joke and I just smile and shrug. I look down at my phone to check a few emails since I have time.

I then look up from my phone to look around impatiently—when a gorgeous chocolate brotha catches my eye. He is having a conversation with a customer. He is speaking, nodding and smiling. Then, he looks right at me! In my mind I can hear D'Angelo's soulful sexy voice singing "Another Life." *"I got a craving for confection so sweet…"* He is the finest man I've ever seen. I am gazing at him. He is gazing at me. He is so attractive, it's actually downright inappropriate! I look off for a moment. Then I glance back and he is still looking directly at me!

He is smiling at me mischievously. I see his confidence, it's very sexy. He's got a fresh half-moon caesar fade, a conservative-sized gold chain on, a well-groomed beard, classic sensible Air Jordans and a blue grocery worker apron on.

Why is he looking at me like that? Why is he so fine? Like fine, fine, FYONE!! Hot damn, where has this chocolate Adonis been all of my life. Good Lord! I can't take my eyes off of him… I feel paralyzed. I cannot stop staring at him and my vagina is throbbing. I feel uncomfortable and swept away at the same time. This eye contact is intense.

I decide to lower my gaze and I just shut my eyes and put my head down. I then find myself in a day-dream with this man that I've just seen. Kissing him passionately, my hands caressing his muscular physique. Ohhh, I know he smells good. I imagine us together intimately. Then I hear a voice.

"Excuse me, ma'am?" the handsome stranger says, as I open my eyes. "Hi!" he says, smiling.

"Hello, um… I ahh… I'm so sorry," I say, shaking my head in disbelief as I snap out of my day-dream fantasizing about him. I clear my throat and look back into his beautiful face.

"It's okay, I can take you over here on lane seven," he says.

"Okay."

"I can take that for you," he says, reaching for my shopping basket.

I release it happily. I follow him to lane seven. I didn't realize that I'd yearn for a physical connection ever again, after chemo and the ordeal with my ex. But I'm feeling him! His name tag says Edward. "So Edward, how are you doing today?" I ask in an attempt to show confidence and decorum, after looking hot and bothered just minutes before.

"I'm doing well," he says, smiling, checking and scanning my items. He calls for his replacement over the intercom after he has scanned my items.

"Okay, that will be $37.63."

"Okay, I'll be using my debit today."

"Okay, you can just swipe when the blue light comes up." He continues to bag my grocery items. His associate walks over. "Yeah, hey Nate, would you take over while I help this young lady to her car?"

"You got it bro!" Nate says, smiling.

"Oh no! You don't have to do that," I say flirtatiously.

"No, I insist," Edward says, fighting a smile.

Whoo, okay! I think to myself as we start toward the exit.

"So you know my name, now I'd like to ask what your name is," he asks politely.

"My name is Jadirah," I answer, as we continue walking.

"Well, it's nice to meet you. Now my next question is, where are we walking to, or did you park all the way out in Africa somewhere?"

We laugh. "I'm parked on the back row here to the left." I point out as we approach my Bentley. As we make small talk on the way to my car, I can tell by his appearance that he is different. That finesse in the way that he talks and moves. The confidence. The definition of confident, smooth and cool. Everything that sistas love, so I know that he probably has a girlfriend. He looks younger than me. Who cares, though? I don't! He is perfection!

I point my car out to him and pop the trunk. He notices. "Woah, okay. The white Bentley! That's you?" he asks, smiling.

"Yeah, that's me!"

"Alright I got you," he says, placing the grocery bags into the trunk. "May I ask you another question?"

"You sure do have a lot of questions. But sure, ask me anything."

"Are you single? And if you are, can I take you out to dinner sometime?"

"I don't know… I mean I'm… ah, not sure, I might be…"

Edward interrupts, "What, you don't date older guys or guys who work at the supermarket? Or is it that you don't date guys who are working on their P.h.Ds?"

"…Edward…"

"Please call me Ed."

"…Okay, Ed, I don't know because I can tell what type of a man you are. You're the type who has a high opinion of yourself. I see a silent confidence and well, great eye contact, and guys like you keep a girlfriend. Trust me, the fact that you work at the supermarket and, I'm flattered, that you think that you're older than me! It's cute," I say with an all-around-the-way attitude.

"Okay, I hear you but peep this, I can tell the type of woman you are. You are the type of woman that I would do anything for."

"Okay is that right? How old are you, 29? 30?"

"I'm 32."

"Okay, I'll take your number Ed," I say, nodding and reaching for my phone. He gives me his number and I place it into my contact list. Who knows who Edward will be in my life, he could be a friend or he could be my peace. "I don't know if I should be taking your number," I say with a raised brow and a smirk upon my face. My flirtatious side is kicking in. I'm so obviously turned on by his presence. "You look like trouble, Ed."

"And you look like you're looking for trouble, Jadirah," Edward says, biting his bottom lip, looking directly into my eyes.

My goodness, this man's sex appeal has me lusting yet again! I snap out of my gaze and resist his charms. "Well…" I begin as I clear my throat. "I have to, umm, I have to get going," I stutter the words out, fighting a smile. I open the door.

"Okay, I look forward to hearing from you very soon, Jadirah."

I wave to him and sit in my car. He stands aside as if he's going to see me on my way. I roll my window down and back out. "Thanks for walking me to my car, Ed."

"No problem at all. Call me, okay?"

I nod and pull off. I head home, ready to see my children. This will be the first time that Carlos will see my new home. We have been meeting up in the city when it concerns the children. Now that the divorce is final, I'm comfortable that we won't end up back in court for anything that I have.

I arrive home and park my car in the garage, grab the groceries out of the trunk and head inside the house in a hurry. Carlos and the children should be pulling up any minute now. I set the grocery bags onto the countertop and, as I'm putting the almond milk away, I hear keys unlocking my front door. It's them. Why do I feel anxious about seeing Carlos? I speed walk to the door and Isaiah is loosening the key from the door.

"Hey Mom! We're home!" Isaiah announces.

We greet one another one at a time, exchange pleasantries and hugs. I look up and see Carlos standing in the doorway. "Hey Jadirah, how are you doing?" Carlos asks.

"I'm doing good! Please come in! Take your shoes off and put them over here please."

"Okay, no problem. Jadirah, you have a very nice place here," Carlos says, placing his shoes beside the door.

"Thank you very much."

"So, the glow-up is a real thing, huh?"

"I feel blessed. God has been blessing me. I'm in remission, just closed on the house... I feel grateful." We pause. He seems as if he's waiting. "Do you want a tour?"

"Yes, I would like a tour."

"Okay, Ava! Zeek! Will you come down and give your father a tour of the house, please?" I call out up the stairs. "I have to finish putting away the groceries. They got you!"

"C'mon Dad, I want you to see my room first," Ava says, grabbing Carlos by the arm.

I continue to put away the groceries until I am finished. I put some music on and sit down in the family room with my cold mineral water. I feel happy. I begin to think of everything that has happened in my life that has landed me here. I am comfortable with my ex-husband roaming around my house with our kids.

I stand to receive them coming down the stairs. I can hear the steps and the chatter. "Thanks guys, I appreciate it!" I say to Ava and Ezekiel.

"Okay, no problem Mom. Can we go out to the pool? Please Mom?" Ava asks.

"Sure go ahead, just for one hour."

"Yes!" Ezekiel says, running back upstairs for his swim trunks.

"Wow, a pool. You got it going on, Jay. A mansion. I see you got your taupe and mauve bathroom happening," Carlos says, rubbing his hands together with a smirk on his face and a slight smile.

"I always wanted a taupe and mauve bathroom," I respond.

"I remember, but now it's your house, you call the shots. I get it."

I simply nod in agreement.

"Well, I'm gonna get going," Carlos says as he turns to walk toward the front door and grab his shoes. As he laces his shoes, I open the door for him.

"Alright, it was good to see you. I'll text you. I'll get the kids Thursday."

"Okay, sounds good."

Carlos walks outside. As I am about to shut the door, Carlos turns to me and has one last question that he feels moved to ask me. He takes a step toward me slowly, almost reluctant to ask. "Jadirah, I have to ask you, okay, I'm just going to come right out and say it..." He pauses and I wait patiently. "... Don't you feel like you owe me an explanation?"

I think about a long, drawn-out answer for him. Something deep that will unlock different chambers of his brain to make him realize some sort of epiphany and go into an awakening. Then I answer him:

"No," I say.

"Just no? That's it?" he says.

"Yeah, I want to do it on my own."

"Okay," Carlos says, shrugging his shoulders and shaking his head, as if I'm being ridiculous. He gets to his car and… he cries. I see it through the window. I understand.

I decide to honor myself with the love that I expected from Carlos. Real love, true love, unconditional love. My name is Jadirah; in Arabic it means *deserving*. I've lived up to my name, finally.

I don't feel sadness for Carlos. I'm actually grateful for the ride. I am happy I've accessed a new way of life, a new light, a new way of thinking. I'm aware of what the blooming feeling has been all this time and now it has blossomed:

Love.

Divine love.

Real love.

Unconditional love.

Unwavering love.

Unfailing love.

Constant love.

Reliable love.

Incessant love.

God's love.

And I *am* deserving. I think I'm in love again…

I am the prototype.

About The Author

Jamilah Ewing lives in Columbus, Ohio with her amazing husband and their four extraordinary children. When she's not writing or taking care of her family, she spends her time working out at the local gym, enjoying caramel lattes, or hanging around in the local record store. *The Prototype* is her first novel.